Don't Sleep

by
Jason A. Spencer-Edwards

JASP Publishing Inc.
Queens, New York

Published by JASP Publishing Inc.
133-16 230th Street, Queens, New York 11413
Email address: jasps@msn.com

Front Cover artwork by Ady Branzei
Back Cover artwork by Shahan Zaidi
Book Cover Design: Garry T. Spoor and Jason A. Spencer-Edwards
Edited by: Betty Dobson, Joseph Tatner, Jason A. Spencer-Edwards
and Kateline Gresseau

ALL RIGHTS RESERVED
Printed in Hong Kong
International Standard Book Number (ISBN): 978-0-9800338-2-3

ACKNOWLEDGEMENTS

First and foremost, all thanks and praises go to God. I would also like to thank Kateline Gresseau, Fay Edwards, Cyril Edwards, Machael Spencer-Edwards and Wayne Alleyne.

I heard a loud knock on my door.

"Who is it?" I answered groggily while looking at the clock on my dresser (5:30 in the morning was way too early to be disturbed) and hoping the person would go away.

"Don't make me break this door down," Mama yelled as I heard her turning the door knob.

I got up quickly because Mama hated when I locked the door, but if I didn't my cat burglar brother (a.k.a. Sticky Fingers) would be all through my stuff.

Dennis didn't know the meaning of personal space. Last week, I caught him looking through my diary.

I thought by stashing it under my mattress it would be safe, but I would have to be much smarter in hiding my things because he was the biggest—and most adept— snooper I knew.

Last week, at dinnertime, Dennis decided to recite my latest entry, which he apparently memorized. In his annoying, scratchy voice, he emoted like he was speaking from a podium.

"Entry dated February 18, 2009. Dear Diary, I saw Lila today. Can anyone say the word ANGELIC? I wonder if it hurt when she fell out of heaven. She was looking more scrumptious than a plate of Mama's barbecue ribs, with macaroni and cheese, collard greens, and some cornbread on the side. I don't know what to do with all these feelings. It's like diarrhea, and I just don't know how much longer I'll be able to hold it in. P.S. She is driving me LOCO. Praying for another encounter, Brandon"

I sat there feeling embarrassed and violated at the same time. I didn't like Dennis broadcasting my business, and Mama's chuckling didn't make the situation any better.

1

Dennis took a bow like he was accepting applause from a crowd. "Thank you, thank you. You are all too kind."

My eyes were glued to Dennis as he took another bow.

"Mama, are you going to let him get away with that?" I gave Dennis the evil eye.

Dennis took another bow and wasn't paying attention to Mama.

"Dennis," Mama shouted, looking in his direction.

Dennis straightened up immediately and began apologizing to me, stuttering over his words.

"Dennis, I don't want any more of your antics. I am going to check on the cherry pie. I'll be right back," Mama said as she headed to the kitchen.

Dennis made sure that Mama was out of sight before sticking his thumbs in his ears and flailing his fingers as he stuck out his tongue.

"You better stay out of my business," I growled.

"You are so sensitive. Plus you'll never get a girl like that, anyway," he said, snickering under his breath. "You have a better chance of seeing Haley's Comet. The next one should arrive around two thousand sixty-one. That's fifty-one years from now. Good luck. You'll need it."

"You think you are so smart, don't you? If you want to live to be nine, you better shut your fat mouth, or I am going to come over there and shut it for you."

"Is that the best response you can think of? Disheartening, bro. Completely and utterly disheartening."

I picked up a piece of cornbread to throw at him and put it down abruptly when Mama returned to the dining room.

She seemed annoyed as she plopped in her seat and directed her gaze at me.

Mama started speaking slowly, but before long she was yelling at the top of her lungs. "You know what, Brandon? Why are you concerned about girls when you should be concerned about your schoolwork? You are about to finish middle school, and high school is going to be a lot more challenging. And then what? Poor high school grades mean limited college choices. The likelihood of having a good life seems unreachable with a limited education. Unreachable. You are setting yourself up to make life real hard. You hear me, boy..."

I was listening all right. All I got from her long winded speech was *blah, blah, blah, blah, blah.*

Mama was really getting on my nerves.

This year, things had taken a turn for the worst. I'd had to tune her out at least five times a week.

I looked over at Dennis as if to say, "You see what you started?"

Dennis loved drama and was smiling like a butcher's dog.

He began adding his own color commentary. "You are so right, Mama. Some people just don't get it. It's like they are sleeping. I'm not. That's why I take school seriously. I totally get it, Mama."

Dennis was an expert at adding fuel to the fire, and that prompted Mama to continue her tirade. She started raising her voice even louder than before, which I didn't think was possible, being that she was already yelling.

"Brandon Stewart. If you think you are going to be taking up space in this world and not achieve anything, you have another thing coming. You hear me? Another thing coming!"

This was the perfect opportunity to tune Mama out. I didn't want to hear that same old tired speech.

I envisioned Lila and me strolling on a white sand beach somewhere in the Caribbean, holding each other's hand.

"I hope you are listening," Mama said, slamming her hand down on the table. "I don't know what has gotten into you lately."

Her hard slam against our wooden table snapped me

right out of my daydream. Talk about bad timing. I was just about to feed Lila some green grapes that I peeled myself.

She dropped the subject when Dennis said, "Mama, I am almost ready to have my own concert at Carnegie Hall. I will give you front row tickets so you can take a lot of pictures as I play my cello in my all white tuxedo with white patent leather Gucci shoes."

Mama smiled and directed her attention to Dennis, who had his arms out for a hug.

"Tell me more, baby," Mama said as she held Dennis in her arms.

"I am going to be the best cellist in the world one day. I see it as clear as a summer's day in the Caribbean."

Dennis was really laying it on heavy.

"Mama, when I am on that stage, I am going to look in the crowd and see you wearing that red dress you bought last year that makes you look like a movie star."

Mama couldn't stop smiling.

I opened my door and saw Mama wearing her hospital scrubs.

"I am going to work early to relieve a nurse that has been on for sixteen hours straight. We could use the extra money. Your brother's cello lessons are costing me a small fortune," she said, looking around my cluttered room. "Have this room spic and span before I get home. It looks like a pig's sty and smells like one, too."

"Yes, Ma'am."

She needed to get her ears checked, because Dennis' playing was atrocious. Mama spent thousands of dollars on cello lessons over the last two years, and Dennis still sounded like a wounded animal that needed to be taken out of its misery.

I had to accompany Dennis to his cello lessons every

week. I dreaded Wednesdays, but what I hated even more was his instructor, Mr. Manning. He was a famous cellist back in the day, and all he ever talked about was "the good old days."

Mr. Manning's favorite outfit was red overalls that he wore every single time we visited him. The outfit looked so dirty that I wondered if he ever washed it, but the worst thing about him was that he had no front teeth; when he spoke, little bits of spit would fly out of his mouth.

Dennis was probably awake and waiting for another opportunity to go through my stuff. I waited until I heard Mama open and close our noisy screen door before I locked my door.

As I lay in my bed, I heard our 1982 Chevrolet Monte Carlo start up, shut off, and start up again. The engine always turned over after the fifth try. Dad was supposed to get rid of the car a long time ago, but he told me that things didn't always work out as you planned them.

I knew Mama was halfway down the block when I heard that familiar screeching noise our car always made when it picked up speed.

I just fell asleep when I heard something hit against my window. It sounded like a twig or something, which I ignored. I was trying to fall back asleep when I heard something louder hit my window.

I got up, went to my window, and peeked through the blinds.

I saw Keshawn looking upwards with a rock in his hand.

"What are you doing?" I yelled as I opened my window.

"Duh. What does it look like? Trying to wake you up."

"Wake me up? Can't you ring the bell like a normal person?"

"Keep your voice down," Keshawn replied, putting the rock down. "Hurry up and get dressed."

I glanced at my clock. It was 6:30.

"For what? School doesn't start for another two hours."

"Does Pops' store ring a bell?"

"Sure does. I'll be down in a few," I replied, quickly shutting my window.

Pops' store had something for everyone.

He sold phone cards, cell phones, video tapes, and music CDs, and he always had the latest movies on DVD (before they hit the theatres). I heard through the grapevine that Pops ran numbers and sports betting out of the back of the store, but I was never in the back so I wasn't quite sure what to believe.

I decided to leave that rumor alone because it was none of my business, but I could see why people would say that. Pops always had the radio on, listening to the previous night's sport scores.

Most kids in my middle school went to Pops' store for one thing: arcade games. Pops had a couple of old school arcade games that he told us were really popular in the eighties: Centipede, Donkey Kong, Ms. Pacman, Q-Bert, and Super Mario Brothers.

Keshawn and I loved Super Mario Brothers, playing it religiously every day for the last month.

Pops put up a new high score, and Keshawn and I were obsessed with trying to take down.

When I opened the side door, Keshawn was fidgeting like he had ants in his pants.

"I've got to pee badly," he said as he held his stomach.

"Use the bathroom in the basement," I replied. "I don't want to wake up my brother."

Keshawn hurried to the basement, and I went to the kitchen.

I was just about to toast a bagel when I heard Keshawn yelling. "I need another roll of toilet paper."

"For what? I just put a full roll in there yesterday. And I thought you said you had to pee."

"Me, too. But I think that my booty has other plans," he replied as the toilet flushed. "I think I overdid it with the burritos last night, and I am having a serious case of WD."

WD? I thought. *What does that mean? Wild Dog? That's not it. Whistling Dixie? That definitely can't be it.*

I became agitated and gave up on trying to figure out the acronym. Thinking that early in the morning was going to give me a serious migraine. I walked to the top of the basement stairs. "What in the heck is WD?"

"It stands for Wet Dookie. The kind of dookie where you wipe your butt around seventy times and it still feels like you need to wipe it some more."

That was way too much information.

Keshawn must have a lot of time on his hands to be naming his dookie.

I went into the closet, found a roll of toilet paper, went downstairs, and knocked on the bathroom door.

"Hold on a second," Keshawn said as I heard the toilet flush for the second time.

I waited patiently by the door.

Before long, it smelled liked something was dying inside my bathroom. The smell was unnerving, and, if it smelled like that with the door closed, I wondered what it would smell like when the door was opened.

"It's by the door," I said as I ran back upstairs, trying to escape the stench.

I heard the toilet flush again.

"Thanks, man. You are a lifesaver. But can you bring me another roll just in case I didn't get it all. I may have another eruption in school," Keshawn yelled as the toilet flushed for the fourth time.

I pretended not to hear him.

"Yo, Brandon, is this toilet paper Charmin? Because it feels so soft on my butt cheeks. The toilet paper in school is mad hard. It feels like you are wiping your booty with sandpaper."

The toilet flushed for the fifth time.

"My house is not a *supermarket*. I am not supplying you with any more toilet paper," I replied.

"Come on, man. You know I'd hook you up if it was the other way around. Boys for life, right?"

"All right, all right. I'll be right down."

As I came back downstairs, I heard Keshawn grunting and groaning like he was having a baby.

I quickly put a roll by the door.

"Before you come out, I recommend—no, scratch that, it is mandatory that you *use the air freshener*," I said as the toilet flushed for the sixth time.

"Don't worry, I got you," Keshawn said as the toilet flushed for the seventh time.

If Keshawn clogged up my toilet will all turds, Mama would be livid, especially if she knew one of my friends was the culprit.

"Ahhhhh, I think I got it all," Keshawn said as he quickly came out of the bathroom, closing the door behind him. "Whatever you do, don't light a match in there."

"You real nasty! Don't be coming to my house blowing up my bathroom," I said as we made our way upstairs.

"Take a chill pill. That's why we are boys, remember. I've got your back, and you've got mine." Keshawn extended his hand out for a high five.

"Did you wash your hands?"

"Do you want to smell?" Keshawn inched his hand toward my face.

"Get out of here with that," I said as I slapped his hand away.

Keshawn rubbed his hand on his nose, took a whiff, and looked at me. "Ahhh, ahh. It smells just like roses."

At first, I looked at him with disgust, but soon we were both laughing so hard that I almost wet my pants.

I toasted two bagels, and we ate them with strawberry jam. Keshawn's stomach never seemed to be full, so I toasted another bagel and watched him practically swallow it whole. I had to make him wash his own plate. When he was finished, we left my house.

The store was a quick six-block walk, and Pops opened like clockwork every day at 6:45 A.M., except for Sunday, when he took a day off for rest. He said even God rested on the seventh day.

Keshawn and I picked up the pace as we got to the middle of my block. When I looked over at Keshawn, I noticed for the first time that he was wearing a wool ski hat.

"Why are you wearing that winter hat? It's mad hot outside."

It's not that hot," Keshawn said, pulling the hat closer to his eyebrows.

"Yes, it is. It feels like eighty degrees already." I watched sweat run off his chin.

"Don't worry about what I am wearing," Keshawn snapped.

I looked to my right as I heard Ms. Reynolds old voice.

"Good morning, Brandon and Keshawn. Where are you both off to so early in the morning?"

"Good morning, Ms. Reynolds," we replied in unison as we stood in front of her house.

She adjusted her thick glasses and looked at her watch. "School doesn't start for another hour and a half."

I didn't want to look directly at her because she was extremely cock-eyed. I couldn't quite figure out if she was looking at me, at Keshawn, or around the corner.

"Cat got your tongue?" she bellowed.

I wasn't quite sure how to respond because, if I didn't answer, she would surely tell her new buddy, my grandfather, who moved in with us a couple of months ago. If that happened, Granddad would be talking to my parents, and then I'd have to answer a boat load of questions.

"We have a talent show coming up, and we are part of the stage crew," I said, fingers crossed behind my back. I hoped she would drop the subject.

Keshawn whispered in my left ear. "Ms. Reynolds' glasses are so thick that when she looks at a map, I bet she can see people waving."

I held my breath for a couple of seconds so I wouldn't burst into laughter.

"We should get out of here," Keshawn said, fidgeting in place. "If we don't hurry, we won't get a chance to play Super Mario Brothers."

Ms. Reynolds slowly walked off her stoop and up to Keshawn.

"Young man, I may be old, but I have excellent hearing. I heard your wisecrack, and, contrary to your belief, I have excellent eyesight, even though I wear these thick glasses," she said as I tried figuring out who she was looking at. "And what I can clearly see is that you are one *ugly boy*. Matter of fact, you are so ugly that you'll never be able to go to the zoo because, if you did, they wouldn't let you leave."

She smiled as I burst out into laughter.

"That was a good one, Ms. Reynolds," I said, holding my sides.

Keshawn was embarrassed but tried not to show it. "Okay, Ms. Reynolds, we will see you later. We don't want to be late."

As we started walking away, she bellowed, "Do you boys think that I am stupid? You are probably going to Pops' store to play video games. I don't know why anyone would want to just sit there punching buttons like a robot. Couldn't you young people find something more productive to do? How about read a book?"

"Read a book," Keshawn repeated.

"Yes, read. You can do that, right?"

"Of course I can."

"That's good to hear," she said as she started walking back to her stoop. "And now that my feet have become swollen, I was wondering if you two wouldn't mind getting me a newspaper."

"Sure, Ms. Reynolds. What paper do you want?" If I said no, I would be up the creek without a paddle.

"Please get me the *New York Post*," she said, still smiling. "Let me go inside and get some money."

I hated taking money from Ms. Reynolds. She was the living embodiment of an old miser, and I felt embarrassed going to the store with the pennies she always gave me.

It seemed like forever as we baked in the sun like chocolate chip cookies in an oven. She was taking her sweet time, and I felt uncomfortable just standing around in that heat. She finally came back outside and carefully opened a brown paper bag.

"One, two, three, four, five, six..." she counted aloud while resting on her stoop.

It seemed like she was stuck on forty for about five minutes. When her phone rang, she stopped counting.

"I'll be back in a minute," she said as she hobbled back inside.

It was way longer than a minute, and I heard her giggling on the phone like we had all the time in the world to wait for her.

"This old fart is taking forever," Keshawn said, fidgeting in place. "Pops' store is going to be mad crowded. We're not going to get a chance to play."

She finally came back out. "What number was I up to?"

"Forty," I said. "Ms. Reynolds, we really have to go."

"Hold your horses. You young people are always in a hurry," she replied as she rested her cane on her stoop. "I just can't take your word for it. My money is really important to me. Let's start the count over, shall we?"

In seemed like hours before she reached fifty.

She carefully handed me a brown bag full of pennies.

Pedro's Bodega was a block away, and when we got there Pedro was behind the counter making sandwiches.

I felt embarrassed as I handed him the brown paper bag full of pennies.

"Can I get one *New York Post*?" I asked, trying to keep a low profile.

Pedro emptied the brown paper bag onto the counter. *"Uno, dos, tres, cuatro, cinco, seis, siete, ocho, nueve, diez..."*

Keshawn looked lost because he didn't understand Spanish; he was taking German and French.

I felt good because counting to a hundred was the only thing I mastered in Mr. Sanchez's class. If he gave us that question on every test, maybe I would be passing his class.

Every time Pedro looked like he was going to be finished counting, he stopped to help customers who were calling out their sandwich orders.

I wished he would hurry up, but customers kept coming in.

I looked at my watch.

If we didn't get out of there soon, Pops' store would be jam packed. I was happy when Pedro finally stopped counting. "Sorry, *amigo*, you are one penny short. I can't give you the paper until you come back with that penny."

I looked at Pedro like he was crazy.

"Are you telling me that I can't get the paper because I am one penny short? You know me. I come in here all the time."

"*Si*. I do see you in here often, but that is not how I run my business," Pedro responded as he slapped some mayonnaise on a customer's hero. "You know what would happen if everyone that came in here tried to stiff me a penny." Pedro took out a calculator. "Let me work this out for you."

I was in no mood to do a math equation.

"Look," he said showing me the answer the calculator displayed. "I would lose thousands of dollars a year if I let everyone slide."

I was heated but left the bodega with the brown bag full of pennies under my arm.

"Pedro is bugging," Keshawn said, staring at his watch.

I looked down and saw an empty soda can on the sidewalk. I took out my frustrations on the can and kicked it into the street. I watched as the can landed on the opposite side of traffic. Maybe I should try out for the kicker for my school's football team.

I looked down at my feet and noticed a shiny penny lying near the edge of the sidewalk. I looked around quickly before picking it up. As I was putting it in my pocket, I saw Christian.

"It's like that," he said as he began laughing. "You that broke that you have to pick up pennies from the street."

"Nah, it's not like that," I said, looking around nervously. "What had happened was—"

"It's all good. I understand. What happens in Vegas stays in Vegas, right? Your secret is safe with me. Scout's honor," he said as he burst out into laughter again.

As Christian disappeared around the corner, I quickly went back into the store. Pedro was still making sandwiches. "Here's is your stupid penny," I said. "Are you satisfied?"

Pedro smiled and said, "*Gracias*. Let's count again."

He slowly emptied the brown paper bag, and all the pennies crawled across the counter.

When Pedro finished counting, he handed me the *New York Post*, and Keshawn and I quickly made our way back to Ms. Reynolds house. She took forever to answer her door.

"I was about to send a search party for you," she said, opening her screen door.

I handed her the newspaper, and she inspected it like she was looking for typographical errors. She opened up the paper and began flipping through the pages. She then read out a headline that she said interested her and closed the paper.

"Thank you, kind sir. Buy yourself something nice with that," she said as she handed me a quarter.

Keshawn started snickering under his breath. "I am quite sure with all that money you can buy a whole lot. Don't spend it all in one place."

"Thank you, Ms. Reynolds. We'll see you later," I said, trying to act like I appreciated her little tip.

I went to close her door when her dog Sasha came barreling through the screen door. She jumped on me and started licking me all over my face.

I looked behind me, and Keshawn was standing frozen like a statue. He never moved when dogs were around because he was deathly afraid of them; even puppies scared him.

Sasha broke loose of my grasp, leaped onto Keshawn, and tumbled onto Ms. Reynolds' grass.

I watched as Keshawn's hat came flying off.

"Yo, who zeeked you," I said trying not to laugh.

"My mother. She said she was going to give me the hottest hair cut anyone had ever seen," Keshawn said, pointing to his head, "and this is the result."

What a disaster! It was more like a science project gone wrong. Keshawn had a light fade on the right side of his head, the left side was completely shaven bald, and the top of his head had several rectangular looking patches that I guessed were supposed to be an intricate design.

Ms. Reynolds couldn't control her laughter.

"And you say that I can't see. Was your mother awake when she cut your hair?"

Keshawn found his hat near the bushes and quickly put it back on his head. "Brandon, promise you won't tell anyone."

"You know you won't be able to keep your hat on in school," I said, trying not to laugh again.

"I already gave this some thought." Keshawn tried to adjust his hat perfectly on his head. "My cousin's a doctor, and I had him write me a doctor's note saying that I have ringworm."

That's what I loved about Keshawn; he always had a bailout plan.

Pops must have overslept because as we came up to his store we saw him opening the door. As usual, he was sporting his blue and orange New York Knickerbockers hat. It was weathered and had holes all over and smelled like vinegar and toe jam mixed together. The hat really needed to be thrown in the garbage, but it was like part of his DNA.

Pops told us that he bought it during the 1969-1970 season when the Knicks won their first NBA championship; after they won their second one in the 1972-1973 season, he saw the hat as a good luck charm and promised himself that he would be wearing it until they won another championship.

Pops must be a glutton for punishment because anyone who knew anything about basketball knew that the Knicks sucked and winning another championship was not going to happen for another million years.

None of us dared say that aloud after what happened to Louis Nelson in Pops' store three months ago.

"What's the definition of a lost cause?" Louis asked loudly. When no one in the store answered, he added with a laugh, "The New York Knickerbockers."

Everyone was shocked, and no one said a word except for Pops, who quickly made his way in Louis' direction.

"I don't ever want you see your face in here again," he shouted as he escorted Louis out of the store.

"I'm sorry. I'm sorry. I was just joking."

"You're sorry, all right. You are officially banned from my store. No one talks bad about my Knicks, no one." Pops closed the door in Louis' face. "Find somewhere else to go, where people find you funny, because I don't."

"How you young fellows doing this morning?" Pops asked as he saw us approaching.

"Everything's good in the hood. What's crackalackin?"

Pops looks confused. "Excuse me if I don't understand what you mean," Pops said, slowly making his way through the door.

Pops was a big man, standing at about six feet four inches and weighing at least 400 pounds.

"I assume that means, 'What's going on?' Or is that some kind of new sandwich."

It was amazing how most conversations with Pops always seemed to have something to do with food.

"It's a fancy way of saying 'What's up?' Pops," Keshawn replied.

Pops let us in and adjusted his pictures on the wall— pictures that showed him in his early twenties, competing in a bodybuilding competition where he took first place in the heavyweight division. Pops used to be ripped. If I didn't recognize the distinctive mole that he had on his right cheek, I would swear that he was lying to us.

Pops turned on the lights, and we welcomed the breeze when he turned on the fan.

Pops perched on the stool behind the counter, and I wondered how it supported all his weight.

"Hey, young fellows. I started my diet last week. Can you tell?" He pointed to his extra large belly, which looked even bigger than last week.

Keshawn and I were in front of the arcade games with our backs turned, trying not to crack up.

"Pops definitely isn't on a diet. It's more like a try-et. Any foods he sees, he always screams, 'I'll try it'," Keshawn whispered in my ear.

I agreed with him 350 percent.

If anything was for certain, Pops definitely had a weight problem; he couldn't wait to eat.

Pops turned on the radio, cranked up the volume, and started singing this awful song.

"Aww sookie, sookie, now!" Pops said, snapping his fingers. "This is called go-go music, and the group is called E.U. Man, when I hear this song I just want to go do some dancing." Pops got off the stool and came out from behind the counter. "Doing the butt. Hey pretty, pretty. When you get that notion, put your backfield in motion...Tanya got a big ol' butt (oh yeah!), Theresa got a big ol' butt (oh yeah!), and Shirley got a big ol' butt (oh yeah!)..."

Pops was gyrating all over the place, and it wasn't even five minutes before he started panting like he just ran five miles.

"Young fellows, I am tired. I need some water then something to eat. I don't move like I used to, but I can still cut a rug. A whole lot better than you young people." He tried drying his face with his already drenched t-shirt. "What is that new dance I seen on TV the other day? Oh yeah, I remember. Spank that soldier boy."

I shook my head in disgust. "Pops, it's *crank* that soldier boy, not *spank* that soldier boy."

"What I know for sure is that boy needs a spanking for polluting my eyes and ears with that stupid dance and song. That is the dumbest thing I have ever seen. That is way too many moves. I've seen fewer moves on an hour-long exercise DVD." Pops began shaking his whole body like he was struck by lightning. "See, when you just do the butt, you can stand in one place and shake your butt like it's on fire. *Now that's dancing.*"

Keshawn and I laughed, and we started imitating Pops

shaking his butt when he went to the back of the store.

Pops came back out shortly.

"Man, I feel ten pounds lighter," he said, rubbing his stomach. "I've worked up quite an appetite. I think I am going to order an extra large pizza with the works for lunch."

"I thought you were on a diet?" Keshawn asked.

"I am. But a little cheating now and again won't kill me. I deserve to celebrate my progress so far."

Keshawn whispered, "Progress. It looks like Pops is regressing. His stomach is way out of control."

Keshawn and I started playing two players for Super Mario Brothers, and I was racking up all the coins on the board. I was surprised that no one from our school was there, and I was happy that we had the game all to ourselves.

A couple of people came into the store and bought chips, soda, candy, and phone cards. Pops was busy arranging CDs behind the counter.

Keshawn and I usually got stuck on the same board, and I popped in some more quarters so we could continue playing. I already spent two dollars.

When I pressed the two player button, I looked over to the door as three people entered the store.

The last person entering the store caught my attention because of his height. He looked about six-foot-nine and had his head bent down low.

He had to be burning up wearing a long black leather trench coat.

Like a jack in the box, he raised his head while putting on a clown mask. "Open up that cash register *now* before everyone gets hurt," the stranger shouted as he positioned himself in the middle of the store.

A lady let out a curdling scream, and Pops quickly turned around.

I didn't actually see a weapon, but the stranger looked

like he was pointing something through his coat pocket.

The robber saw Pops easing in his direction and quickly moved towards Keshawn and me.

Keshawn dropped to his knees. The robber grabbed me in a headlock and pushed me hard to the floor.

I fell to my knees. He pulled me up by my neck, and I felt something poking in my side. "I want everyone to move to the back of the store, especially you, fat boy. Don't try to be a hero. Everyone to the back *now!*"

So many thoughts were running through my head as we headed to the back of the store. Should I fight for my life, or should I just comply with his demands?

This was becoming a movie scene I wanted to skip.

I looked over at Keshawn for a sign. He always knew what to do, and I always counted on him to have an answer. He looked empty inside, so I decided that I didn't want to play the hero and be the only one killed.

"I want you all to stay in here, or else you'll be pushing up daisies," the robber barked as he left us in the back of Pops' store.

It was five of us packed in a tiny bathroom, like sardines in a can. I didn't know whether to cry or hold my nose, because the bathroom still reeked of doo-doo.

I wished Pops used the air freshener that I noticed was still wrapped in plastic, sitting on top of the toilet tank.

I started praying silently, and Keshawn still looked like he seen a ghost. I heard the cash register open and things being moved around in the front of the store. This lasted for a few minutes then I heard the front door being slammed closed.

No one knew if it was safe enough to come out, but Pops told us that he wasn't going to stay in the bathroom forever. He opened the door and went to the front of the store.

Everyone came barreling out of the bathroom, and we were heading to the front of the store when we heard Pops scream.

"That punk took all my money, CDs, DVDs, cookies, soda, and potato chips, too," Pops said with his hand over his forehead.

He was so mad that it took him a while to call the cops.

The store looked like it was hit by a hurricane. Pops would be cleaning everything up for hours.

Keshawn and I were in no shape to go to school.

One of the ladies who were in the bathroom with us began hyperventilating, and it took a while before she calmed down. Keshawn still looked like a deer caught in headlights, and he had a huge pee stain in the front of his pants.

We left Pops' store and headed back around the way.

I was happy that we made it out of Pops' store alive.

Dennis was eating a big bowl of Frosted Flakes at the dining room table. "What are you doing home?" he asked as I walked past him. "Did you forget your brain and come to see if you could find it?"

I completely ignored him and made my way through the living room.

Granddad was relaxing on the vibrating La-Z-Boy chair that we got for my father on his birthday.

"School is going to be starting in about half an hour. What are you doing home?" Granddad said as he changed the TV channel.

"I can't go to school today," I answered with my head down. "I was in Pops' store and it got held up and the robber grabbed me and I thought he was going to kill me and everybody else in the store."

"That store is trouble with a capital T. Pops got all kind of stuff going on in the back of his store. How many times did I tell you to stop hanging out there?" he said, changing the channel again. "A hard head makes for a soft behind.

You hear? A hard head makes a soft behind."

What about showing some empathy? I thought. I was almost a goner, and all I got from Granddad was a lecture. I wished he would stop talking.

"Brandon, your head is as hard as steel. You need to put your thinking cap on," he said as he changed the channel for the third time.

I decided to tune him out like I usually did with Mama.

"You better call your mama now," Granddad yelled when he noticed I wasn't paying attention. He handed me the cordless phone, which he always kept on his lap so he wouldn't have to get up when the phone rang.

It was like someone pressed the on switch on a Tickle Me Elmo doll after I told Mama what happened.

She went ballistic and started screaming.

"I can't believe your stupidity. I have had enough of your antics. You think you can disobey my rules like you are a grown man. You aren't grown yet. You're still under my roof. Keep this up…"

I thought she wasn't going to stop and felt relieved when she told me that she was just paged.

I hung up the phone, went straight to my room, and snuggled under my covers. Before I closed my eyes, I set my alarm clock for 4:15 P.M.

My alarm went off as scheduled, and I quickly went into the bathroom, brushed my teeth, gargled with some mouthwash, and made sure there was no sleep in my eyes.

I carefully brushed my hair to the front, to the back, to the left side, then to the right side, hoping that I was creating some waves.

After a few more brushes and checking my hair at every angle in the mirror, I realized I was wasting my time. I didn't have what Grandma called "good hair."

I looked at my watch and hurried outside. It was 4:28

P.M.

I jetted to the backyard, grabbed the broom, and went to the front of my house. I started sweeping, even though there wasn't anything to clean up.

A minute later, Lila came walking up the block.

I soaked up every bit of her beauty as she approached.

Lila was twenty-three years old, five-foot-ten, and had an hourglass figure, long, black wavy hair that went down her back, and a blemish free, roasted hazelnut complexion that matched her hazel eyes.

A man driving some expensive looking convertible was staring at Lila so hard he almost hit a parked car. Lila was the living embodiment of the idea that beauty could stop you in your tracks.

I knew I didn't have what it required to take her out or be her man, but I still had a crush on her.

"Hi, Brandon," Lila said as she stopped right in front of my house.

"Hi, Lila." I walked up to her to get the hug she always gave me.

Every day, I looked forward to that hug, and, even though it was more like an older sister hugging her little brother, I was still thankful to be that close to her. I didn't want to let go. I had my eyes closed, and I was taking in the scent of her perfume.

My experience was interrupted as I heard Keshawn shouting, "Hey, Lila."

I opened my eyes and saw Keshawn sprinting up the block like a cheetah.

When he got in front of Lila, she smiled, let me go, and shifted her full attention to him.

He was cutting into my Lila time.

"Hey, Keke," she replied as she gave him a bigger hug than she gave me.

Where was my nickname?

I watched as Keshawn held onto Lila as if he was

hanging on from the edge of a cliff for dear life.

My jealousy cup was about to overflow.

Lila's cell phone rang, and she answered it. She got caught up in her conversation and soon afterwards she was saying goodbye to the both us.

Keshawn was still cheesing as he kept his eyes stuck on Lila as she crossed the street and headed up the block.

"Why didn't you call me and tell me Lila was around the way," he said watching her as she almost moved out of our sights.

He knew the rule: *if you snooze, you lose.*

"It slipped my mind," I replied, fully knowing that I had no intention of sharing the Lila experience if I could help it.

Keshawn and I sat on my stoop, and he still had that stupid smile on his face.

"Did you hear Lila say that I had a cute hat? I think she is digging on me."

I laughed so hard that I almost fell off my steps. "You don't have a chance."

"Maybe not. But you don't, either."

He looked at me strangely. "Don't move."

"Why? Do I have a bee on me? You know I hate bees."

Keshawn went into his pocket, took out tweezers, and picked at something on my shoulder.

"Got it."

"Got what?"

Keshawn went into his back pocket and took out a Ziploc bag.

"One of Lila's hairs. It's only a matter of time before they start cloning human beings. And then I can use my savings to create my own Lila with this strand of hair."

"Man, you have been watching too many sci-fi movies," I said, still looking up the block even though Lila was out of sight.

I glanced at my watch. It was almost 6:00 P.M.

"Keshawn, peace. Mama will be home any minute."

"Peace out, I'll check you later," he replied as he got up and headed down my block.

I heard the wooden floor creak in front of my room and knew it had to be Dennis. He had a habit of listening at my door.

I slowly got up and tiptoed to the door and quickly opened it. Dennis came crashing forward into my room.

"Stop snooping. You little busybody."

"I wasn't snooping. I was just seeing if you were here. I heard you were in Pops' store when it got robbed. Were you scared?"

"Nah, I wasn't scared. I was about to beat the robber up, but Pops stopped me. You know my hands could be a registered weapon."

"Do I look drunk? You couldn't beat an egg properly."

I had enough of his smart mouth, and I escorted him out of my room by his collar. When he was outside, I smacked him in the back of his head.

"Awww, that hurt. I'm telling Mama."

"So tell her, you little tattletale. You think I am going to get a beating. I am too old to get a beating."

"So you're too grown to get a whooping, huh?" Mama seemed to come out of nowhere. "Don't try me, young man. You are still on shaky ground."

"Hi, Mama," I stuttered. "I was just playing around."

Mama looked beat. She gave Dennis a kiss on the cheek, walked by me without responding, and went to her room, closing the door behind her.

I went back inside my room.

It was so humid upstairs. I wished I had an air conditioner in my room like Dennis had. But those things were "extras," and I didn't qualify to get any of those "special amenities" until I brought up my D- average to at least a B+.

I heard something crash against my window as I tried relaxing on my bed. I went to the window, opened it, and saw Keshawn.

"Yo, you want to go to the ave?"

"You crazy? My mother is home. I'll speak to you tomorrow."

"All right. Peace. I'll check you tomorrow."

I went back to my bed and tried making myself comfortable by lying on the top sheets to escape the heat.

My neck was irritating me.

I got up and looked in the mirror and saw that it was red from where the robber had me yoked up like a helpless baby. I put some lotion on it, hoping to soothe the pain. It wasn't working.

My father popped up in my head as I looked at the walls.

We painted them together when we first moved into our house. I missed him badly, and I wondered when he was coming home. Dad seemed to like his job. I hated everything about it, but Mama told me that was the life of a truck driver, on the roads day and night for months at a time, picking up and delivering things.

Dad's old job was way better because he was at home every night, and I missed being able to talk to him anytime I wanted. He didn't deserve to get fired because of what Mama called "office politics."

I reached under my bed and grabbed the box that held all my postcards. Dad always sent me postcards when he got to a new state, and I always wrote him back.

I really looked forward to his postcards because he wrote more than he called.

The last one I got was a month ago.

Hey Brandon,
    Arizona is really hot. And I think I saw the devil

wearing a bikini. Anyway, I have a load to take care of, and I miss and love you guys. I was at this hotel and they had this saying on a plate that I thought was interesting. Tell me what you think.

Instead of counting minutes, make your minutes count.

Take care
Love always Dad.

I awoke to the sound of something hitting my window.

I wished Keshawn would get it through his thick skull that he should ring the doorbell.

I opened my window and gave him a tongue lashing. He just smiled. After listening to his pitiful apology, I told him I would be down in a minute.

I came outside, and Keshawn had a bunch of quarters in his hand.

"Let's go to Pops' store to play. My treat," he said, flipping a quarter in the air.

"Are you crazy? I don't want to ever step in that store again."

Keshawn started laughing. "Come on, man. I want to take that high score down badly," he said, adjusting his hat. "And you know the saying: lightning doesn't strike in the same place twice."

"Let me think it through first."

"What is there to think about? Just go with the flow. Be spontaneous. Check it, we'll only play two games. I promise," Keshawn said as he flipped a quarter in my direction. "Plus, I have a science test that I can't miss today, and I am trying to get to school early to get the answers from a student that took it yesterday."

"I still don't know, man."

"What are the odds of Pops' store being robbed two days in a row? Don't even give this a second thought. Let's just go to Pops' store and take down that high score."

Keshawn was usually right in situations that could be tricky. What idiot would try to rob Pops' store again after the cops started patrolling the neighborhood more frequently since yesterday.

28 Don't Sleep

Pops was at the counter rearranging CDs. "What's popping?"

"Where'd you learned that slang from?" I asked, looking at Pops weirdly.

"I am just trying to connect with you young people. We used slang back in the day, too," he replied as he munched on a jelly donut. "One I still use to this day is, 'Don't sleep.'"

"Don't sleep," we replied, knowing that it couldn't be the literal meaning.

We struggled to follow what Pops was saying when he went into this long explanation and started to tune him out. "Metaphorically speaking, sleep represents awareness of the environment or surroundings you co-inhabit with other cats and foxes. But keep your eyes peeled because if you don't, you'll get caught with the ookie doke. And no one likes getting caught with the ookie doke. You dig, youngsters?"

Say what? Was Pops talking another language? Keshawn and I looked at each other then directed our attention to Pops.

"Yeah, we got it," we both lied so Pops would stop talking. We resumed playing Super Mario Brothers, and we were on a roll. We reached a level that we never got to before.

I turned around as the door burst open.

"Don't move. And I mean *nobody*. Give me all the cash, and this will be over quickly."

Keshawn and I quickly put our hands in the air.

Pops looked disgusted. "The money is in the cash register. Just take it," he said as he began walking towards the robber.

I didn't see any weapon, and I wondered if the robber was bluffing. I think Pops read my mind because he lunged at the guy and clipped him like he was sacking a quarterback.

Pops caught the robber off guard, and a tussle ensued on the floor by the door. Pops was punching the robber to his midsection, and the robber was trying to defend himself by punching back. I couldn't tell who was winning because Pops' big frame had the robber totally eclipsed.

I wasn't sure if I should jump in or wait to see what was going to happen next. I looked over to Keshawn for a sign, but he still had his hands in the air.

It was unbelievable.

The robber somehow flipped Pops off him. That's when I heard Pops scream. He rolled over onto his side. The robber rushed out the door.

Keshawn and I ran over to Pops, who was still moaning in pain and clutching his side. As we tried getting him up, we saw his shirt was stained.

Pops was bleeding.

We struggled to sit him upright. He was way heavier than he looked, and I wished that he was further along on that diet.

"Pops, are you okay?" I said, still trying to move him.

"Hey, young fellow," he said faintly.

Keshawn and I decided that moving him wasn't a good idea. Keshawn went to the back and got a towel. As I applied pressure to the wound, Keshawn called 911.

"Hey, Pops, how you feel?" I asked.

"I guess I was wrong, huh?" Pops said, wincing. "He did have a weapon, and a sharp one, too."

"Pops, you are real brave," I replied, applying more pressure to his side and slowing down the bleeding.

"Did that thief get any money?" Pops tried to sit up.

"No. He left out of here, running for his life."

"Good. That's good," he replied as his eyes rolled to the back of his head.

It seemed like an eternity before the ambulance arrived.

The police came in first and took statements from us as the EMT workers put Pops on a gurney and quickly took him away.

We weren't able to give the cops much information because the robber was wearing a mask. The only thing I told them was that he might be the same person that robbed the store yesterday; both robbers were unusually tall.

As Keshawn and I walked back home, we were dead silent. When we got in front of my house, I told Keshawn that I would see him later. He mumbled something under his breath as he walked slowly down my block, his head still down.

I barely had the strength to put my keys in the door. I fidgeted with the lock a couple times before I got inside.

I went to the basement and saw Granddad taking a load of clothes out of the washing machine.

"What's wrong with you, boy?" He looked at his watch. "You should be in school already."

As I began explaining to him what happened, he just shook his head. "Why can't you listen? How many times have I told you not to go in that store? What do you think Pops does in the back?"

"That is a rumor, Granddad. Plus, no one has the right to rob people like that. That punk needs to be taught a lesson."

"There are a lot of people in the cemetery who tried playing the hero. Do you want to end up like them?"

"Well, I'd rather die fighting like a man than die like a coward."

Granddad did something that he never did and got so close that I felt his straggly beard on my face.

I backed up.

He pulled up his shirt. I saw a long, keloidal scar that went from the top of his chest all the way to his belly button.

"That was from playing the hero. I don't tell you a lot about me because there are a lot of things that I am not proud of," he said as he pulled his shirt down. "I got that trying to take a knife away from this guy who was trying to rob me and my friend. I was in the hospital for two months, and all this happened because, when we were being held up, my friend mumbled that he thought I could take him. He was way bigger than me, and I should have used my own judgment. Back in those days, I was a follower, being led by friends I thought knew better than me. Just like a sheep."

I didn't really care what Granddad said because he was way out of touch as far as I was concerned. He spent most of his days watching television and, lately, talking on the phone with Ms. Reynolds. I thought he was just using her to replace the memory of Grandma, who was Granddad's whole life. When she had a heart attack and died five years ago, I think a piece of him died that day, too.

I tuned Granddad out as soon as he started telling me that I wasn't focused enough. It was like talking to Mama all over again. I started to go upstairs when my Granddad called me back downstairs.

"Where are you going?"

"To my room. I don't feel like going to school."

"You think you have the luxury of just staying home? Boy, get a move on."

"Don't you see that my hands are still shaking? I am in no shape for school today."

"Nonsense. It will stop. I can take you to school myself," he said with a broad smile. "Give me ten minutes."

I weighed my options and figured if I said no he would tell Mama, and I was already in hot water.

"Fine."

Granddad was ready in under ten minutes.

"Granddad, what are you wearing?" I said, giving his

ensemble an inspection. He wore red corduroy pants, a white sweater with a purple shirt, a gold tie, and a pair of green pointy-toe boots. His afro was as white as snow, matching his white beard with connecting sideburns.

"Clothes, silly," he said, adjusting his pants.

He looked like a cross between a Keebler elf and Santa Claus.

"Aren't you going to at least comb your hair?"

"Nope."

"Granddad, you look like a ghetto Santa Claus."

"On the contrary, Brandon. I can only look like myself," he replied, smiling away. "I feel very comfortable in my skin. Haven't you ever heard that it's what's on the inside that counts?"

I continued pleading with him to at least do something with his hair. After I practically got on my knees, he went upstairs and quickly came back down.

"It took me a while to find it. Do you like it?"

Granddad had on this awful straw hat that resembled what the scarecrow had on in *The Wizard of Oz*. I thought he looked absolutely ridiculous.

As we walked out the door, Granddad grabbed his yellow umbrella.

I felt embarrassed getting on the bus with him, and I was fortunate that no kids from my school were anywhere in sight.

The ride was pretty fast. As I got off the bus, I saw Christian and a couple girls that were in my homeroom class walking toward the front steps. I guessed they were late, too, and I tried hurrying up the stairs so they wouldn't notice us.

It was as if Granddad was purposely taking his time.

I heard one of the girls snickering and saw her pointing at my grandfather.

"Granddad, could you pick up the pace a little?"

He ignored me and took his sweet time as he gingerly

walked up the steps.

He came to a halt when he saw a penny. He picked it up, inspected it for a few seconds, and put it in his pocket. He was smiling away like he just found a valuable artifact that was lost for centuries.

"This must be my lucky day," he yelled as he stood still in his tracks.

Christian and the two girls, who were directly behind us, laughed so hard that I thought my eardrums were going to burst.

Granddad was family, and I didn't appreciate them laughing at him. I turned around and gave them one of my best screw-faces.

Everyone stopped laughing except for Christian.

I wanted to sock him in the mouth, too, but that would be like a chihuahua picking a fight with a pit bull. Christian was at least five inches taller than me and outweighed me by at least seventy-five pounds.

We reached the security guard and, after Granddad signed in, went to the main office for a late pass.

I made my way to math class and said goodbye to Granddad, who was just smiling away like he wanted to come with me. He could be very weird sometimes.

I was trying to figure out what was on the board when I felt something hit my head. I turned around and saw Christian snickering. I looked down to the floor. Next to my desk was a shiny penny.

A couple more people in the back row started laughing.

By the time our math teacher, Mr. Rose, turned around from the blackboard, everyone had their heads buried in their books, pretending to be copying the **DO NOW**.

Mr. Rose adjusted his glasses, quickly turned back around, and continued writing on the board.

I rubbed the back of my head a couple times before

copying the **DO NOW**. I could hear whispers coming from the back of the classroom. I looked to the back and saw Christian whispering something to Mariah Morgan.

Mariah had her face all contorted as she leaned on his desk, carefully listening to every word.

"That is too funny. Could you repeat that again?"

Mariah then looked at me and shook her head.

Could life be any crueler? I thought as I turned back around.

Mariah was the gossip guru for our school, and boy was she efficient. She actually had a team of workers. It could be text messages, word of mouth, or her own daily blog from her website where she broadcasted the latest school gossip.

Any information she got was pipelined to the rest of the school in a matter of a school period.

I couldn't concentrate.

I wished I could somehow be able to alter time and erase the whole day, because in one measly class period (forty-five minutes) I would be packaged, sealed, and delivered to a location where all the losers in our school resided: Outcast Avenue.

I looked at my watch. Time was speeding along; for the first time this school year, I wanted the clock to actually stop working.

I took in a couple deep breaths.

Maybe I was jumping the gun. I shouldn't just assume that they were talking about me. They could be talking about anything. Besides, Christian and Mariah didn't say my name once. Trouble was pure speculation on my part.

That comfort was nullified as I heard Mariah laughing again.

I looked to the back of the classroom, and Mariah was still laughing. I watched as she began writing something down on a piece of paper.

She neatly folded it in half and passed it to Gerald

Wallace.

He looked at it, looked at me, laughed, and passed it to his left to Marsha Fields.

It was happening right before my eyes, and I wanted to intercept the note, but if I got out of my seat, Mr. Rose would be calling my home, and I didn't want to fail his class for the second marking period in a row.

The note continued making it rounds.

Carol Whittaker had the note in her hands, and I immediately wanted to cry. The first day of school, I had asked her to the junior prom, but I still hadn't received an answer. She knew I still wanted to go with her because I had Keshawn remind her about it a month ago.

Carol looked at me long and hard and gave me the worst screw-face I've ever seen in my life. It read disgust personified. At that moment, I knew that my opportunity was incontestably ruined.

I turned back around, feeling like the biggest loser in the world. I didn't want to look around the classroom anymore because every few seconds I heard someone new giggle. I tried blocking out the laughter, but it was hard.

It wasn't too long before I felt another stinging sensation. I rubbed my head as I looked down and saw another penny on the floor. I quickly turned around.

Christian was laughing like something tickled his fancy. "Aren't you going to pick it up? You know how much you and your family like pennies," he said, loud enough that most people could hear, except for Mr. Rose, who was still writing on the board.

I stared at the penny then picked it up and put it on my desk. The whole class burst into laughter, and that's when Mr. Rose turned around.

"What's so funny? I like to laugh, too, but when it's appropriate," he said, looking at his calendar on his desk. "But let me also remind you that you'll be having a quiz by the end of the week. So focus, young people, focus. Your grades are your own responsibility."

Mr. Rose continued writing on the board, and I could still hear Christian's repulsive laugh.

I closed my eyes and took in some deep breaths. I couldn't drown out the snickering.

I started rocking back and forth, trying to calm myself down. It wasn't working. I heard more snickering.

I had had enough.

In one quick motion, I picked up the penny, aimed it, and threw it in Christian's direction.

Bull's eye! I caught Christian in his left eye.

Mr. Rose turned around after hearing Christian howl in pain.

"Brandon Stewart. Are you working with a full deck? March yourself right to the principal's office."

"For what? Christian threw a penny at me first," I yelled.

"Are you unable to use that thing that is stuck between your ears? Why can't you seem to be able to think things through? I guess you really don't want to graduate, huh," he responded as he began writing a pass.

"I didn't start it. It was Christian who started it."

"I don't have time to figure this out, so I want both of you to go to the principal's office. *Now*."

Principal Jones hated to deal with any drama, so he was not happy to see us.

"Why today? My horoscope said that I was going to have a smooth day," Principal Jones said, closing his newspaper. "I need an explanation as to why you are both here."

"Christian threw a penny at me, and I threw it back," I said, watching Christian as he covered his left eye. "I didn't want to hit him. I just wanted to get his attention."

Christian didn't utter a word. In this case, silence

wasn't golden. He was going to tear me limb from limb as soon as he got better—that's if he didn't get someone else to do it for him.

"Is that the best you can come up with?" Principal Jones said as he took out my folder and wrote something inside. "I want both of you out of my office. And consider yourselves lucky that I can't verify what happened. If I could, I would suspend both of you. But one thing I know for certain is that I will be calling both your parents."

Principal Jones called his secretary and told her to bring him my blue card. In less than five minutes, he had Mama's work number. When he began dialing, I became squeamish.

I let out a silent sigh of relief when I heard him say, "I'll try back later. Thank you very much."

I looked at my watch and realized Mama was on her lunch break. Talk about good timing. Principal Jones then called my house and, after a quick conversation, told me that my grandfather was on his way to pick me up.

The secretary couldn't find Christian's blue card, and Christian told the principal he was having trouble remembering his parents' numbers. Christian was good at lying. His facial expressions told me he was going to pummel me into next week.

Principal Jones escorted me to the bench outside of his office and told Christian to go to the nurse's office to get his eye looked at. I sat on the hard metal bench, waiting for Granddad to arrive.

An hour passed before he strolled into the office. He was wearing that same outlandish outfit, and I felt embarrassed when a couple of students came into the office and asked if we were related. I wanted to say no, but Granddad called my name out so loud that there was no denying the truth.

Granddad was in the principal's office for about an hour before he came back out and signed me out of school to go home. The bus ride was quiet, and I was wondering what was going to happen when Mama found out.

As soon as I got home, I went to my room and lay on my bed. I was about to close my eyes when I remembered that I didn't set my alarm clock.

I quickly set it for 4:15. Seeing Lila would be the only bright spot after my disastrous day.

I was jolted out of my sleep when I heard banging on the door.

"Have you seen my cello?" Dennis said through the door.

I got up but didn't open the door. "How would I know? You need to look for it yourself. Go away," I screamed.

"Mama said you should help me look for it," Dennis replied as he tried opening my door. "But it's okay, you don't have to help me. I'll just call Mama and tell her."

I got up quickly and helped Dennis find his cello, which was always in the same place, under his bed.

I went to the kitchen to get something to eat. I made two tuna fish sandwiches with mayonnaise, bacon, tomatoes, and sweet relish. I enjoyed every mouthful and washed the food down with my favorite drink concoction: orange juice and fruit punch mixed half 'n half.

I was washing the dishes when I heard my alarm going off. I ran upstairs and saw that I was behind schedule. It was 4:42. I grabbed my sneakers and darted outside. I looked up the block and saw Lila.

I could have kicked myself. Lila was already a block away, and she was not alone. I stared harder and recognized Keshawn's ugly wool hat. He was practically attached to her side, and Lila even rubbed his hat a couple times.

I sat on my stoop, annoyed.

It seemed like Keshawn was hanging out with Lila forever. When he came back to my stoop, he was all wide eyed.

I wanted to smack that stupid smile off his face. "Why didn't you come and get me?" I screamed.

"You know the rule: if you snooze, you lose," he replied as he sat next to me.

Lila's perfume still lingered in the air, and I knew he had to get an extended hug for it to be still so strong on his person.

"You are the talk of the school, homey. Everyone is saying that you are mad poor. So poor that you and your family have to pick pennies off the street to pay your bills," Keshawn said, not really looking at me. "You know Christian started that rumor, and when Mariah got hold of it, you know it was a wrap."

I nodded and realized that I had no chance of taking Carol to the school dance—and probably any other girl for the rest of the year.

"Don't sweat that," Keshawn said, trying to cheer me up.

He jumped off my stoop and kneeled next to my bushes, his fingers behind his ears like he was trying to hear something.

"What are you doing?"

"Keep it down," he whispered as he got closer to the bushes. "I am calculating the temperature by listening to a cricket."

"Calculating what?"

"Check it. I heard you can tell the temperature in degrees Fahrenheit by listening to a cricket chirp. I am going to count the number of chirps in fifteen seconds and then add thirty-seven."

"Have you lost your mind? Where did you hear that mumbo jumbo?"

He ignored me and started counting chirps. "It's eighty-seven degrees outside. If you don't believe me, check it out for yourself."

He was bugging. This was my opportunity to clown on

him. I went inside and checked the Weather Channel.

I couldn't believe that he was right.

I came back outside and sat next to him.

"I was right, huh?" he said, looking up the block.

"Yeah. So what?"

"I told you."

"I didn't need to know the exact temperature. By the sweat running off your forehead, I could tell that it's mad hot outside," I said as I began to laugh. "You are sweating like a fat person in a donut shop."

"Hardy har har."

"How much longer do you have to wear that stupid hat?"

"The doctor's note my cousin gave me has me covered for two more weeks." He wiped sweat off his face. "Plus, my mom just got fired, and money is tight. I won't be getting a haircut until we get some extra funds, and I don't know how long that will be."

"Sorry to hear that, homey," I said, putting my hand on his shoulder.

I looked at my watch. It was getting late, and Mama would be home soon. I was about to go inside when I saw Granddad strolling down the block. That was unusual because Granddad was carrying a couple plastic bags and he usually didn't venture too far from the house.

"Where've you been, Granddad?"

"Hey, young fellows," he said, stopping in front of the stoop and putting his bags down. "I went to Jamaica Avenue to pick up a couple of things." He searched through one of his plastic bags and handed me a neon pink sweatshirt with red writing on it.

I looked at it and wanted to puke. On the front of the sweatshirt read "Down the Rabbit Hole." When I turned to the back, I saw a big red bunny.

I quickly handed it back to him.

I wanted to tell Granddad that he was getting weirder

by the hour, but he seemed so pleased with his purchase.

"That's cool, Granddad," I said as I tried acting excited about his purchase.

"I'm glad that you like mine. I bought you one, too. This is in honor of one of the best books in the world, *Alice's Adventures in Wonderland.* Remember when we read it together a couple of years ago?"

I didn't know why he was excited about fairytales and make believe things. I hated that stupid story, and I didn't remember most of it, but what I did remember was that it wasn't real. The next thing I could look forward to was Granddad convincing me that the Boogey Man was real and lived up the block.

"I also bought this movie called *The Matrix.* I've never seen it before, but the guy told me it was good," he said, searching through another plastic bag.

I took a look as Granddad handed me a VHS tape.

VHS tapes were archaic. I tried explaining to him that most people purchased DVDs because they had excellent picture quality, interviews with actors and directors, and deleted scenes and alternate endings.

Granddad didn't seem impressed and told me he wasn't into all that technology and what he purchased was good enough.

Keshawn looked at his watch. "Yo, I am going to check you later."

Granddad and I went inside.

I was pouring myself a glass of lemonade when I heard the phone. I picked it up on the third ring.

"Yo, Brandon."

"What's up, Keshawn?"

"Mariah just called me and said that Christian was talking about your family again, saying that your father was in rehab for drugs and alcohol."

"Why is he lying? He's never even met my father."

"That's the same thing I told Mariah," Keshawn

replied. "It took me a while, but I convinced her to give me Christian's number. I just got off the phone with him. I told him that he better keep your name out of his mouth."

"You did what? You know Christian will cut your head off first and mine second. I don't need any more drama."

"I told Christian that he was a hater and that I had a perfect solution to squash this little beef."

I was listening and wondering what Keshawn had in mind.

"You are to meet him at the YMCA on Parsons and Archer."

"For what?"

"I told him that you challenged him to a race in the pool. If you win, he will give you two hundred dollars and leave you alone. And if you lose, you will give him two hundred dollars."

"Are you crazy? You are literally throwing me to the sharks."

I had heard that no one had ever beaten Christian in a pool race since kindergarten, even then he had raced against older kids.

Besides he was our swim team captain and had more medals than days in the year.

Keshawn said, "The whole school is practically going to be there. Even Carol Whittaker."

"Did you say Carol Whittaker?"

"Sure did. I am almost sure if you won she would definitely go to the prom with you."

I was sold, hook, line, and sinker.

I went downstairs and found my swim trunks then grabbed my keys and headed out the door.

I was halfway down the block when I heard Dennis screaming, "Mama's on the phone."

I quickly made my way back to the house. "What does she want?"

"I'm not psychic. You speak to her."

Mama told me that she was working late and that I should drop Dennis off at his cello lesson.

I waited for Dennis to get dressed, and we got on the bus to Jamaica Avenue. Keshawn was sitting next to me, and we weren't really paying attention to Dennis.

"You know Christian doesn't have a chance of beating you."

I looked at Keshawn blankly.

"If you can see it then you'll believe it, and then you'll achieve it," he chanted. "If you can see it then you'll believe it, and then you'll achieve it."

Keshawn sounded crazy at first, but the more he said it the more I started believing. Then he started a new chant. "Every dog does have his day, and today is mine for the taking. Every dog does have his day, and today is mine for the taking."

I felt empowered, and I began barking like a dog that was ready to pounce on anyone or anything in his path. People on the bus were looking at me like I was crazy, and Dennis was shaking his head.

When we got to the YMCA, Keshawn, who always had the hook-up, finagled three free guest passes for us. Keshawn and Dennis made their way to the swimming pool area, and I went into the locker room. I quickly undressed, put my stuff in a locker, and made my way to the pool.

Christian had major pull. Since he knew the lifeguard, the pool was empty, but the bleachers were packed. It seemed like the whole school was in attendance. I made my way to the middle of the swimming pool area, and everyone in the bleachers was quiet.

Christian emerged from the lifeguard entrance, and two giddy sixth graders began screaming his name when they noticed him. The crowd caught on and began cheering and clapping like Michael Jordan just arrived. He wore a black swim cap with his initials showing on the side, black swimming goggles, and black Speedos.

All the females in the crowd were gasping for air when he began posing like a bodybuilder. He took his sweet time positioning himself in front of the diving board. The crowd was still cheering and clapping, and he was enjoying every second of it.

I was already in front of my lane and wanted to get this race over with as quickly as possible.

Christian raised his left hand, and everyone got quiet.

He pointed to the bleachers, and Mariah Morgan emerged through the sea of people with a microphone in her hands. "Testing one, two, three. Testing one, two, three," she said as she began playing with the microphone.

Mariah introduced herself to the crowd, even though she didn't need to. There wasn't anyone in our school who didn't know who she was. She introduced Christian, and the crowd went bonkers again.

He looked over at me and winked.

The pressure was getting to me. I felt like I was going to have an anxiety attack.

The last time I was in the water was seven years ago when our family went on vacation to Antigua. Dennis was just a baby, and I felt good beating my father to a boat that was about 200 yards from the shore.

But that was ages ago, and Christian took swimming a lot more seriously than my father. I closed my eyes for a second and thought, *Why am I racing him?*

Mariah introduced me to the crowd, and I only had two supporters. Dennis and Keshawn were hooting and hollering like deranged lunatics, and Dennis was jumping around like he had ants in his pants. I appreciated his support, but I knew he was just glad to be around people that were older than him.

I looked around the bleachers for more support. The person I wished was clapping for me was Carol, but she wasn't even paying attention. She had her head down, and she appeared to be texting someone.

I looked over at Christian.

"See you at the finish line, chump," he snarled as he waved to the crowd of people, who began cheering his name again.

Christian's confidence rattled my cage, and I didn't feel brave enough to tell him to eat my dust even though that would be the perfect way to play mind games with him.

Mariah bellowed into the microphone, "On your marks, get set, GO!"

I dived in, and when I surfaced saw that Christian was at least a full body length ahead. I started kicking my legs and moving my arms in and out of the water as fast as I could. I splashed water everywhere as I tried to push my body forward as quickly as I could muster.

I got halfway down the pool and noticed I almost caught up to Christian. I was really winded and started breathing heavier after each stroke. I kicked a little harder. When I looked over to my right, I noticed we were neck and neck.

Everyone in the gym was quiet, and I wished I had goggles like Christian's. The water was getting into my eyes, and I could feel the sting of chlorine.

I got to the end of the pool, touched it, flipped underneath the water, and came up for air just like the Olympic swimmers did on TV.

I looked to my right again. I couldn't believe Christian was two full body lengths ahead now. I obviously didn't execute the flip thingy correctly.

I heard the noise of the crowd. They started chanting, "Christian! Christian! Christian! Christian!"

I began kicking even harder, and I was halfway to the end of the pool, but I was still behind. My arms, legs, and chest were burning, but I kept pumping away. I didn't open my eyes to see where Christian was; if I wanted to catch him, I had to concentrate.

It seemed like I was swimming for hours until I finally

hit the end of the pool and came up for air. I looked over to the left just as Christian slammed his goggles into the water.

I wiped my eyes and noticed that people in the bleachers were church quiet. The crowd looked dumbfounded.

I won! I was on cloud nine. I felt like David who slew the mighty Goliath.

I quickly got out of the pool and pumped my fists in the air like professional athletes did on TV. Then I began my slow victory walk around the pool, strutting like a proud peacock.

I looked to the crowd, craving support, and spotted my two staunch supporters. Keshawn and Dennis' energy was intoxicating, and they were carrying on like I just won an Olympic gold medal.

Everyone else in the bleachers was in total shock, and there were so many open mouths that I wished a swarm of flies would perch on their tongues.

I looked to the bleachers again and spotted another fan.

Carol Whittaker was clapping louder than Dennis and Keshawn put together.

Our eyes met, and she waved to me.

I had a Kool-Aid smile on my face as I slowly strutted in Carol's direction, making sure that Christian could see where I was heading.

I stopped in front of Carol, and she handed me a perfectly folded piece of paper—the same piece of paper that I gave her on the first day of school. I quickly unfolded it and looked at it carefully. Carol had the YES box checked. That meant she would go with me to the prom.

That was the proverbial icing on the cake, but I was far from full. I wanted another slice of ecstasy.

It felt good hearing my name. It was the sweetest melody I heard all year. Dennis, Keshawn, and Carol were my personal cheerleaders, and they made me feel so good as they continued screaming and clapping.

I pointed to Keshawn and winked at him, which was our little signal, meaning "good looking out, homey." I was so glad that he talked me into racing Christian. I owed him big time.

I continued reveling in the moment as I went around the swimming pool for another victory stroll. Christian was so mad that he was practically foaming at the mouth.

"A penny for your thoughts," I said as I purposely brushed past him. "Speaking of pennies, how do you want to pay me? If you want to pay me in pennies, it will be twenty thousand."

It was as if steam was coming out of Christian's ears.

I brought my attention back to my three supporters as they started chanting, "Brandon! Brandon! Brandon!" I decided it was time for me to bust a move, and I started dancing. Pops would have been proud if he had seen me shake my booty.

It wasn't too long before I felt a spine tingling chill. I stopped moving, looked down, and saw that my swimming trunks were at my ankles.

Christian looked pleased. "Ooops, my bad. How clumsy of me. I really didn't mean to do that. I am so so so sorry."

The bleachers erupted in laughter except for Carol, Dennis, and Keshawn. And I sure didn't find anything funny about me looking like a total herb.

Christian was trying to catch his breath as he continued cracking up. He went over to Mariah Morgan and took the microphone from her.

"You are even lamer than I thought. I can't believe you are fourteen years old and still wearing Superman underwear," Christian announced as he urged the crowd to repeat after him. "Up in the sky, it's a bird, no, it's a plane. No, it's Superman."

I struggled to pull my swimming trunks up; as I did I

tripped over my feet and fell into the water. I felt even more embarrassed as I struggled to get out of the pool.

Christian yelled, "I thought Superman could fly. I guess not. I guess you had a dose of kryptonite. Your name should be Super Lame."

As the crowd continued laughing, I began searching in my head for answers. I started replaying what I did in the locker room earlier, and that's when things became clear.

That was my ah-ha moment.

I was in such a hurry that I forgot to take off my underwear before I put the rest of my clothes in the locker. How stupid of me.

Christian and the crowd were chanting in unison. "Up in the sky, it's a bird, no, it's a plane. No, it's Super Lame."

The laughter was deafening, and I needed someone else to blame. The only person that came to mind was my father. He knew that I loved comic books. And if, while he was on the road, he found underwear that had comic book characters on it, he would send it to me. He told me that I could make believe that they were protecting me when I felt lonely or scared, but that was supposed to be our little secret.

I quickly made my way to the men's locker room as the crowd continued laughing. Soaked, I sat on the bench and didn't want to move. I covered my face in my hands. I was in the dumps as I searched in my mind for a silver lining for my situation.

It wasn't too long before I came up with something. At least I still had my underwear *on*. If not, I would have been as naked as a newborn baby. Then the constant ridicule I would have experienced would have had me transferring to another school for sure.

I still heard the crowd chanting, "Up in the sky, it's a bird, no, it's a plane. No, its Super Lame."

I opened my locker, got my stuff, and began getting dressed. As I was putting on my sneakers, Keshawn came into the locker room.

"Are you all right?" he asked as he put his hand on my shoulder. "No matter what people say, you'll always be cool."

Dennis was right behind him. "Yeah, bro. Anyone that laughed at you needs to grow up. Especially Christian. He's a big time hater."

I grabbed my stuff and headed outside. The first person I saw was Carol. She was talking with some of her friends as I approached. Dennis and Keshawn stayed a distance back.

When I reached her, she handed me a piece of paper with my name on it.

"Should I open it now?" I said with a smile.

"It's up to you," she responded as she returned my smile.

I unfolded it like a man that knew he was about to get rewarded for his bravery and service to mankind.

In big blocks letters the note read:

I AM SORRY THAT I'LL NOT BE ABLE TO MAKE IT TO THE JUNIOR PROM. I DECIDED TO GO WITH CHRISTIAN.

I felt as if someone ripped my heart out of my chest and stomped on it. I balled up the piece of paper and threw it onto the ground.

I walked over to Keshawn and Dennis and told them I didn't want to talk when they began asking me questions.

Keshawn looked at his watch. "Yo, I'm about to be out. I'm going to handle some business. I got mad chores that I've been neglecting."

Dennis and I walked three blocks north of Jamaica Avenue to Mr. Manning's apartment building. I pressed 4B on the intercom and waited for Mr. Manning to buzz us in.

That was an excruciating experience. He treated everyone like they were the Seventh-Day Adventists.

Ten minutes later, I heard his hoarse voice. "Can I help you?"

"Yeah, you can you buzz us in," I replied in a smart tone.

"Who's us?"

"Brandon and Dennis," I answered, knowing that he knew my voice.

"Who?"

"Brandon and Dennis. Let us in. We've been waiting for a while."

"What's the rush? Take your time, young man. Give me a second."

We waited a little bit longer before he buzzed us in. We got on the elevator and pressed the button for the fourth floor.

I rang his bell and waited for him to come to the door. I started getting impatient, and I wondered if he went to sleep or was in the shower.

I heard footsteps approaching the door. I put my eye to the peephole and could see another eyeball staring back. I knocked on the door this time.

Mr. Manning screamed, "Hold your horses."

He had four heavy duty security locks on his door, and he always struggled with the last one before he let us in. As he opened his apartment door, I recognized his favorite outfit. *What a surprise,* I thought. When would he throw away those dingy, smelly overalls?

I could smell the incense he loved to burn and hear jazz music in the background.

"Come on in, boys. Give me a second to turn down the music."

I was glad that he did because that music sounded depressing to me. I couldn't do any kind of dances to it.

Mr. Manning never played hip-hop music because he

said that any fool could put some nursery rhymes together, sell it to the public, and claim to be a musician.

I sat in the living room as Dennis practiced the cello in a room in the back. For the life of me, I didn't quite get why Mr. Manning and my parents bothered. Couldn't they hear that Dennis wasn't getting a lick better?

When they took a break, Mr. Manning came into the living room with some apple juice and a plate full of oatmeal raisin cookies. He set them down on the table and left.

I bit into one and quickly spit it out. It was as hard a rock. I felt like I chipped a tooth and looked in the mirror on the wall to check. Everything looked fine. He was lucky.

If I had chipped a tooth, I would have sued him.

He must have had these cookies for years, I thought as I picked up another one and struggled to break it in half. I quickly put it back on the plate.

Mr. Manning shouted from the back room, "Aren't those oatmeal raisin cookies the best you ever had? I can bring out some more, if you like."

I wrapped up the evidence in a napkin and put it in my back pocket. I didn't want to offend him. "I'm good. I'll just finish what's left on the plate."

I wished Mr. Manning had a TV in his living room or anywhere else in his apartment. Instead, I sat bored silly on his ugly purple couch that had the stuffing coming out of all sides.

My mind went back to Christian; he ruined my swimming victory, ruined my chance with Carol, and had the whole school talking about me and my family.

I wasn't going to be able to get any cute girls to go to the prom with me now. Not even the homely looking girls would go out with me after seeing my Superman underwear. I had a better chance of seeing a flying pig.

I was getting angrier by the second.

I looked around Mr. Manning's living room, trying to

focus on something else, and noticed huge plastics jugs filled to the brim with pennies. What was up with all those insignificant pennies? Did every old person in the world get together and say, "We are going to collect pennies?"

I closed my eyes and fell asleep from straight boredom, but woke up when I felt Mr. Manning shaking me.

He began telling me about Dennis' progress, and little bits of spit flew out of his mouth. Some landed on my cheek and on my shirt. I could be an advocate for the expression, "Say it but don't spray it." I needed a hockey mask just to carry on a conversation with him.

I was happy when his phone rang and he stopped talking to me to get it. Any longer and I would be so wet that I wouldn't need to take a shower.

Dennis was lugging his cello behind him as we exited Mr. Manning's apartment. We got on the elevator, and shortly afterwards we were outside. Dennis stopped at the corner before we crossed the street. He saw a penny on the sidewalk, picked it up, and put it in his pocket.

"A penny a day will keep the hunger away," he said with a smile on his face.

"Where did you get that stupid saying from?"

"Granddad."

"Stop picking up pennies, you are embarrassing me."

"Don't tell me what to do. I can do as I like. Besides, it's worth something."

"You're right. It's worth a grand total of one cent."

As we approached the corner of Parsons and Jamaica Avenue, I saw Christian and some of his boys standing in front of the McDonalds.

Christian spotted me. "Up in the sky, it's a bird, no, it's a plane. No, it's Super Lame."

Christian and his boys started laughing, and I wanted to punch their lights out, but the odds were against me.

"Where is my two hundred dollars?" I shouted.

Christian looked confused. "What two hundred dollars?"

"The two hundred you were supposed to give me after you lost our bet."

"What bet?" he replied, looking at me like I was crazy. "I didn't bet anything with you."

"Keshawn told me he spoke to you, laid down the terms of the bet, and you agreed on everything."

"I have no idea what you are talking about." Christian turned his back to me. "If you want money, go pick up some pennies. Look over there, I see one on the other side of the street. If you hurry, maybe no one will notice it."

Christian and his boys started laughing again as he pointed across the street.

"Shut up, you ugly goat," Dennis said, pointing at Christian.

"Who you calling ugly, shorty?"

"You. Matter of fact, you are sooo ugly that people put your picture in their car window as an anti-theft device."

Christian's boys laughed, and he started moving towards us.

"You better tell your brother to shut his mouth before I shut it for him."

Dennis was a major pain in the butt most of the time, but he was the only brother I had. For once, I didn't mind that he was running his mouth.

"Christian, do me a favor and please close your mouth, because your breath smells so bad that people look forward to your farts."

I held my sides as I started cracking up. I thought I might pee myself.

Christian's face turned red. "You know what? Yo mama!"

"I am going to take the high road. I won't say one word about your mama, because her *face* says it all," Dennis replied with a devilish grin on his face.

Christian's boys laughed even harder, and he swung at Dennis.

Dennis ducked, and I jumped in front of him.

"If you put a finger on my brother, and I will tear your head off."

Christian laughed. "Are you serious? Or maybe you got a penny stuck in your brain and it needs to be jarred a little."

"Try me and see what happens," I said with my fists clenched.

Christian cracked his knuckles. When he cocked his left hand back, a security guard from McDonalds came outside.

"If you kids don't move along, I am calling the police," he said, twirling his flashlight.

Dennis and I moved across the street, and Christian and his boys followed close behind. I was almost at the end of the crosswalk when I felt a hard push. I tumbled forward and fell onto Dennis.

"Ooops, I have to work on my clumsiness. I *really* didn't mean to do it," Christian said, laughing as he stepped around us and continued walking with his boys.

What a mess! Dennis' cello was crushed.

Dennis was speechless. I saw tears in his eyes as we started picking up the pieces that were scattered all over the sidewalk as pedestrians walked around us. It was like a jigsaw puzzle that no one would be able to figure out.

As we picked up the last piece we could find of his cello, the only thing that came to my mind was that his carrying case provided no protection whatsoever.

"I'm going to be in big trouble." Dennis wiped his face with his t-shirt. "Mama is going to kill me."

"Don't worry about it, she'll just buy you another one."

"Another one? That one cost over two thousand dollars," he said, sniffling.

"Everything will work itself out. Trust me."

Dennis loved to exaggerate. I was sure that Mama could get him one for less than a hundred dollars.

I thought it would be a quiet bus ride home, but Dennis was animated nonetheless.

"I'm pretty funny, huh?" Dennis said, fidgeting in his seat.

"You got some okay jokes."

"*Okay jokes?* I was roasting that fool like Mama's stuffed chicken. I could be a professional comedian, selling out shows across the nation." He cleared his throat. "Check this joke out: Christian's Mama is so ugly that every time she walks by the bathroom, the toilet bowl flushes."

I laughed so hard that everyone on the bus was looking at us.

"I was just getting started, and I was about to get Christian with some of my most potent jokes. He didn't stand a chance," Dennis said as he stood up.

Then he entertained the bus passengers the rest of the way home.

Mama wasn't home. Dennis let me go into his room to use his computer while he showered. I entered "cello prices" in the search engine and located his model. I looked at the screen carefully to make sure I wasn't seeing things.

Dennis was right.

I went back to my room and lay on my bed, racking my brain on a way to come up with more than two thousand dollars in two weeks. I couldn't think of anything and looked at my clock. It was 6 p.m. I went downstairs to give Keshawn a call. If anyone could know what to do, he would. I told him to meet me around the corner in ten minutes.

He was chilling near the stop sign by the time I got there.

"How much longer do you have to wear that stupid hat?"

"Not that much longer." He adjusted his hat above his eyebrows. "So what's cracking?"

He started speaking slowly and precisely after I explained my dilemma.

"I got a plan," he said, smiling. "I got a real good plan."

I waited quietly for him to spell it out.

"Everyone loves candy, right?"

"Right," I answered, wondering where he was going with the conversation.

"Well, I went with my mom to pick up her last check about an hour ago. And I moved some boxes of Snickers, M&Ms, Mounds, Skittles, and some other candies and put them in her trunk. I figured they're like a parting gift from the job that I helped myself to. We can sell them in school."

"Why would anyone buy candy from us when they can buy it from the store?"

"This is a simple case of supply and demand. First you have to have a quality product that tons of people look for on a daily basis. We have that product—candy, under market price—thus allowing us to sell it for a cheaper price than all of our competitors. That will allow us to practically eliminate all competition, invariably causing the general public to purchase said product from us at a lower price, making us the number one supplier. This will automatically increase demand of said product, due to the fact that we fully cater to our customers' needs, ultimately supplying reasonable and quality products the public will enjoy."

"Say what?"

"Maybe you need for me to speak a language you can understand. We are going to be selling individual candy bars for sixty-five cents apiece. And no tax, either, beating out the price from all the stores, which usually sell them for a dollar or a dollar five apiece. When you add tax, I believe it is about a dollar nineteen or something close to that."

"Sounds confusing."

"Wake up, man. Plain and simple. Everyone will buy candy from us, and we are going to get *pzzaid*." Keshawn sounded pleased with his plan.

"*I like the pzzaid part.* So we split everything fifty-fifty?"

"Are you crazy? How about seventy-thirty?" Keshawn looked up the block. "It's my stuff, plus my mom just lost her job, remember. I need a lot more money than you do."

My parents couldn't afford to cough up that kind of cash, and I didn't have any money of my own or any way to get that kind of bread before Dennis' next cello lesson.

"I'm in," I said, realizing I was in between a rock and a hard place.

"We'll start tomorrow," Keshawn said, giving me a high five. "Oh yeah, before I forget. I need to stash the candy at your house."

I followed Keshawn to his house and noticed that his front yard hadn't been mowed in weeks. We went along the side of his house to the backyard. We picked up five garbage bags and went back to my house, where we hid everything in the garage. No one except my father went in there. Since he wasn't going to be in town anytime soon, our hiding space was secure.

Every teacher who saw me in the hallway stared at me like I had two heads.

I walked with a bop in my step. My heavy book bag appeared to be stuffed with books. I usually brought a basic black, one-subject composition notebook and a yellow #2 pencil stuffed in my left back pocket.

Little did they know my book bag was stuffed with candy that would be soon converted into cold hard cash.

I felt like a salesman in the playground during lunchtime as I tried to unload candy. I set up shop behind the handball courts, where our lunch monitor didn't go unless someone got hurt. That didn't happen frequently, and only the extremely accident prone kids screamed out when they were hurt. And if they did, they usually wished they didn't say anything because gossip traveled fast in school and they would get clowned on for at least a month.

My first customer was Mariah Morgan. She was the co-sign I needed. Mariah and her cohorts spread the word faster than a forest fire on a windy day. Students were coming over to the handball courts like rats attracted to the scent of cheese.

It was as busy as a flea market…non-stop selling for about thirty-five minutes. I kept reaching into my book bag as kids asked me what kind of candy I was selling. I probably opened the bag about a hundred times. I never thought I'd see the day when Mariah Morgan's big mouth would come in so handy.

When Christian approached me to buy some candy, I gave him a dirty look. I wanted to tell him to take a long walk off a short pier, but Keshawn stressed that the only people we were not to sell to were the adults.

Christian pulled fifty dollars out of his wallet. "Give me whatever that can buy."

I was having a problem figuring out how many pieces I should give him and started counting on my fingers.

"You are taking forever," he yelled as he saw me struggling. "Are you stupid or something?"

I felt embarrassed as I saw Mariah Morgan behind him.

"Christian, take it down a notch. It's not that serious," she said, looking at him funny.

"You better have my stuff when I come back," Christian said as he walked off.

I felt relieved as Mariah helped me count out seventy-six pieces of candy.

Five minutes later, Christian was back with a big plastic bag. I handed him the candy and his change.

"Keep it," he said as he tossed the coins back in my direction. Then he positioned himself in the middle of the playground, where most of the kids were still playing. He handed out candy to anyone who came near him. When other students caught wind of what was going on, they started yelling his name so they could receive candy, too.

Students were flocking to him and I wished I didn't sell him any candy. I was angry, but I calmed down as I realized that I was doing all this stuff for Dennis.

Christian would do anything to make himself look big, I thought. His popularity chart just got a super boost, and everyone would be talking about that for at least a week.

By the end of the week, I sold seven hundred dollars worth of candy.

I met up with Keshawn at his house. His grass was still unkempt, and I wondered if he realized that it looked like a forest was growing in the front yard.

He eventually came to the door, wearing his pajamas and his wool hat.

I gave him a high five then handed him the money.

He counted it slowly and did the same exact thing another five times.

"You did a good job," he said, smiling. "Here is two hundred and ten dollars."

"That's it?" I said, not taking the money from his hand.

"Thirty percent. Just like I said from the get go."

Math wasn't one of my better subjects. And I sucked at calculating percentages. I wasn't too happy because I thought it would be more.

"Are you sure that's thirty percent?"

"Do you want the money or not?"

Time was running out for me, and I really had no other alternatives. I reluctantly took the money.

"Brandon, let's celebrate. I want to cop some new clothes or maybe a pair of sneakers."

I put my hand in my pocket and rubbed the money in between my fingers. I needed to save all my money for Dennis' cello. I had no intentions of getting fresh.

"Nah. I'll pass."

"Come on, man. You going to leave me hanging," Keshawn said then started counting his portion of the money out loud. "That's the least you can do. You don't have to buy anything, just roll with your boy. Just do some window shopping. You know it's boring just staying at home."

He was right. I would probably just go to sleep, and window shopping never killed anyone before.

We grew tired of waiting for the bus so we got on one of those dollar vans that drove down Merrick Boulevard and sat in the last row. The driver, whose speech gave away that he was Jamaican, blasted some reggae tunes. He drove down Merrick Boulevard like a maniac, and I was happy when we got off in one piece.

We walked up two blocks to a strip where all the sneaker and clothes stores were located. It was real close to the Coliseum, which was kind of a flea market/clothing and sneaker store spot.

As we walked past one store, an older looking guy with a mouth full of gold teeth said, "We got sneakers in the back. Exclusive, baby, for thirty."

"Nah, man, we good," I replied, staring at this shady character who looked like he wasn't selling anything authentic.

I soon got bored going from store to store.

Keshawn tried on about fifty pairs of sneakers and still didn't find anything he liked. He seemed to enjoy pissing off the store owners by trying on different sizes then saying that they weren't comfortable.

He looked at me funny when I wouldn't even spend money on food, but he ordered a Philly cheese sandwich with extra onions, extra cheese, onion rings, and a super-gulp grape soda at a broken down looking joint.

He took a huge bite of his sandwich. "Aren't you hungry?"

"I can't afford to spend a penny."

"A penny, huh?" He pointed to several pennies that lay on the street. "You sure you don't want to pick any of them up? There is probably about a hundred of them lying around."

At that point, I didn't want to hear about or see another penny ever again.

"I need some real money and fast," I said as he slurped on his soda. "Do you have any other ideas?"

He didn't seem to hear me as he focused on his sandwich. "You sure you don't want any? You don't know what you are missing."

"I just told you what I should be worrying about."

"All right, all right. Calm down. Let me think about it. But right now, let me enjoy my food. This is way too good to be interrupted."

I looked around and saw the waitress running back and forth from the kitchen, picking up orders. She was flat out busy, and I wondered how much she made in tips as she picked up some money that was lying on the table in front of her.

Keshawn finished his food, and we continued walking along the strip, heading towards the Coliseum. We went into a jeans store, and he tried on ten different pairs. I was happy when we finally left.

We must have stopped in about ten more stores, and he still hadn't bought anything.

We were at the end of the strip, about to enter the Coliseum, when I noticed a guy who looked like he was in his mid twenties eyeballing us from across the street.

Keshawn was too busy looking at two girls who were way out of his league to notice.

"Yo, I think dude across the street is going to roll up on us," I said as I snapped my fingers in front of his face to get his attention.

Keshawn looked in every direction and replied, "Who are you talking about? I don't see anyone."

I didn't see any trace of the guy, either—as if he disappeared into thin air.

We entered the Coliseum and went straight to another sneaker store. Keshawn tried on eight more pair of sneakers and still came out of the store empty handed.

As soon as we got outside the Coliseum, that same guy who was staring at us from across the street earlier on was there, sitting on a car.

I got a real good look at him. He had on all this expensive looking jewelry and was wearing a limited pair of Jordan's I saw on EBay for seven hundred dollars.

He made eye contact with Keshawn.

"What up, yo? Ya'll looking to cop some sneakers for cheap?"

Keshawn looked around and replied, "Why, you got the hook-up?"

"No doubt," he said as he adjusted his diamond bracelet.

"Can you get me the sneakers you have on your feet in a nine and a half?"

"No doubt," he replied as he made a quick phone call. "Follow me."

I wasn't getting a good vibe from him. As he walked ahead, I whispered into Keshawn's ear, "This isn't a good idea."

"Don't be a worry wart. What could possibly go wrong?"

"A lot of things."

"Survey the scene. The odds are in our favor. If he tries anything, it will be two against one."

Keshawn had a good point. The guy was about five-foot-five and really frail looking. We were both over six feet tall and weighed more than him; even if we had to sit on him, he wouldn't be able to get away.

As we continued following behind him, he nervously looked in every direction. It seemed like a long stroll, and I counted block number five when he stopped in front of a store that had apartments on the top floor.

We walked up the staircase, and everything looked pretty clean inside. He knocked on apartment number one, and a fine looking girl opened the door.

Keshawn couldn't control himself. "How you doing, Ma?"

"I'm fine," she said, smiling. "Come on in and make yourself comfortable."

She brought us to the living room, where you couldn't miss the flat screen TV that had to be at least fifty-two inches.

We sat on comfortable, burgundy leather couches that matched the carpet and the drapes.

The guy we came with went to the back of the apartment as Keshawn and I watched TV. The girl sat across from us with her legs crossed, and we both were taking in her perfume.

I was playing it cool, but Keshawn was to trying to give her his "player's eye," which really looked like he was having a bout of Tourette's Syndrome. She looked worried and asked him if he had something in his eye. And if he needed to blow it out, she would help him. I wanted to laugh, and I think he got the picture because he suddenly stopped.

Ten minutes later, the guy came out with a box that contained the sneakers. Keshawn tried them on.

"Yo, these are hot. How much you want for them?"

"Give me a C note," he said as he looked past me to the girl.

"Bet," Keshawn said as he pulled two fifties from his pocket and passed them over.

We had everything we needed, and we started to get up when I saw the guy reach into his pocket.

He took out a switch blade, and the girl had one, too.

Before I could react, she was behind me with the switchblade resting against my throat.

"What's the deal?" Keshawn yelled as he inched toward me.

"Fall back, before Tasha cuts your boy's throat."

Keshawn didn't move another muscle, and the guy went through his pockets slowly.

It wasn't too long before he located the wad of money.

When Tasha saw the money, she screamed, "Jackpot. A sucker is born every day."

She still had the knife to my throat as she began going through my pockets. It felt weird being searched like that, but I didn't want to be cut.

She took everything I had.

They double checked our pockets for any more money

before escorting us downstairs.

When we got outside, Tasha put the knife across her own throat and said, "If you talk, those will be the last words you ever say."

Keshawn had his head down, and I was so mad that I started yelling at him.

"I told you I didn't want to come to the avenue. Now we have no money and no more candy to sell. Why do I listen to you? What am I going to do now?"

"My fault," he said in a low voice. "You know I'll think of something. I just need some time."

"I don't have much time, remember?"

"Have I ever let you down before? Just trust me."

We started walking towards where the dollar vans were. Luckily for me, I had two-fifty in quarters that they didn't find stuffed in the bottom of my shoe, or else we would have to walk six miles to get home.

I woke up after I heard banging on my door. I opened it to see Granddad in his favorite pink long johns.

"You are going to sleep your life away. Don't you see the time?"

I looked at my clock. With less than twenty minutes to get to school, I didn't have enough time to brush my teeth or take a shower. I went to my closet and pulled out the nearest outfit, put it on, and ran out the door with a banana in my hand.

My luck was running at an all time high; as I sprinted up the block, I saw the bus waiting there. I jumped on and was so tired from tossing the night before that I quickly fell asleep.

I got to school as the late bell rang for homeroom.

Most people were talking about their weekends, and I just wanted to go back to sleep.

One of Christian's boys, who normally never spoke, came up to me. "You got any more candy?"

"Nah. I may have some tomorrow," I said as I saw the disappointed look on his face.

I liked the idea of being known for supplying kids with a sugar fix instead of being the fourteen-year-old boy who wore Superman underwear.

That experience was short lived as Christian popped out of nowhere in the hallway after homeroom. "It's a bird, it's a plane, no, it's Super Lame," he yelled, and everyone in the hallway started laughing.

At the moment I felt insignificant, and I wished that Christian didn't go to my school anymore.

Mr. Rogers, my social studies teacher, had already filled the entire board with DO NOW items.

I was still exhausted from not getting any sleep the night before and didn't feel like dealing with another boring lesson. I had little chance of passing his class after receiving an F on his last test. I put my head down to rest my eyes for a moment, and it seemed like only a minute before I felt someone shaking me.

I picked up my head and saw Mr. Rogers standing over me with his lesson book in his right hand.

"So, Mr. Stewart," he said, poking his ruler in my side. "Please explain to me what the 'Arms of Morpheus' means."

I wiped my eyes and looked around the classroom as everyone snickered.

"The only Morpheus I know is in that movie *The Matrix*; I didn't see it, but I know he is one of the characters."

"What a surprise." He shook his head. "Where is your homework on Greco-Roman mythology you were supposed to hand in today?"

I looked in my book bag, pretending to search for it. "Sorry, Mr. Rogers, I must have left it at home."

"You are a real comedian." He looked through his black leather binder that he used to keep our grades, attendance, and class participation. "You have not handed in one homework assignment all year." He closed his book and walked away. "Put your head down. You've been sleeping all semester. The Land of Nod is calling you."

Everyone laughed, and even though I had no idea who and what he was referring to, I knew I was the object of his ridicule.

I sat upright and listened as Mr. Rogers began teaching his lesson. "'The Arms of Morpheus' is a figure of speech known as an idiom. It is a term used to talk about sleeping and/or dreaming."

He took a long pause, and I wanted to rest my head on the desk again, but he was watching me like a hawk.

"In Greek and Roman mythology, Morpheus was the god of dreams, and he would come into your dreams when you were sleeping. His father Hypnos, or Somnus, was the personification of sleep, and he had a twin brother Thanatos, who was the god of death."

Brian Sampson, who loved anything that dealt with history, raised his hand. "Mr. Rogers, the word morphine is derived from Morpheus. And hypnosis must be derived from Hypnos. And a boss you have to fight in *Resident Evil: Survivor* is called Hypnos T-Type. And Hypno is also a Pokemon that is proficient at putting other Pokemon to sleep. And in *God of War: Chains of Olympus*, Morpheus is mentioned as an antagonist. And in *World of Warcraft*, a dragon named Morpheus protects 'The Dreamer' in the Sunken Temple. And insomnia is a sleeping disorder named after Somnus..."

Brian kept regurgitating information like he was prepared to talk for the rest of the period. How could one person remember so much stuff?

"Very good, Brian. But I'll have to take your word when it comes to the video game and Pokemon thing. I don't have time for such things." Mr. Rogers opened his book and took out his pen. "I will give you two points for class participation."

I decided to give it a try and show Mr. Rogers what I knew about sleep. "Mr. Rogers, is it not also true that sleeping is an important factor in how long you can live? Sleep is the gas that fuels your brain and your body. And when you get enough sleep, you feel revived, energized. Sleep boosts your decision making skills and improves your memory. So, in summation, one can draw upon these undisputable facts that one should always get enough *sleep*."

Mr. Rogers looked shocked that I knew anything about

sleep and its benefits. I would have to thank Mr. Curry, my
gym teacher—who smelled just like his name—for making
me memorize all that information just to pull out a sixty-
five in his class last semester.

"Bravo, Mr. Stewart," Mr. Rogers said as he clapped
three times. "In that case, you should be energized every
day; even when your eyes are open, you are still very much
asleep." Then his tone became more serious. "What you
should be doing is paying attention to what's going on
around you. You are failing my class again. And what high
schools have you even applied to? Don't you know that if
you don't graduate high school, your chances of being
successful are diminished? And those who don't graduate
high school are eight times more likely to end up in prison.
Is that where you want to be?"

I didn't answer because I had to listen to that prison
speech since the third grade. Adults just said that to scare
you. People broke the law every day and got away with it. I
never got arrested a day in my life or found myself in a
situation that I felt would land me in what Mama called
"the big house."

I would have appreciated if someone had come into our
classroom and arrested Mr. Rogers for exposing a minor to
his constant badgering. He was boring me to death. I
wondered if he had kids and what they thought of him.
When the bell rang, I was happy to be done with his class.

I saw Keshawn in the hallway.

"I was throwing rocks at your window for about fifteen
minutes. What happened to you this morning?"

"I was knocked out."

"I've thought of a way to make some money," he
whispered, like anyone was paying attention to us. "I'll see
you after school."

"All right, cool," I said as I made my way to English
class.

I was happy that we had a substitute teacher. They

didn't teach much because no one ever listened to them, and they were usually afraid of us. Everyone pretty much did what they wanted. I sat in the back of the classroom with my eyes closed, sleeping until the class ended.

I met up with Keshawn at lunchtime, and we sat at the far end of the cafeteria. I didn't say too much because I was still tired. I ate our school's Sloppy Joe sandwich even though it looked like dog food. I was so hungry that I ate Keshawn's lunch, too, when he didn't want it.

At the end the day, security guards directed kids to go straight home. I hated how rude they usually got. I moved along quickly, though; getting caught hanging around school premises would mean automatic detention for a week.

Principal Jones instructed the security guards to enforce the no loitering policy after school since some boys who didn't go to our school got into a fight. One person got stabbed and was paralyzed for life. Another one ended up in the cemetery.

I walked over to Keshawn, who was standing at the curb in front of school.

"I got a plan. Follow me," he said as we headed up the block.

"Where are we going?"

"Relax," he replied, looking around. "We are going to get more money. Have some trust in me."

We got on the bus and were both quiet as the bus rolled along.

He was still wearing that wool hat and was sweating profusely. I wondered if someone's head could explode from extreme heat. I got bored watching him and fell asleep.

I felt Keshawn nudging me. I wiped my eyes and realized we were at Green Acres Mall.

"You want to go shopping at a time like this?" I said as I got off the bus. "I'm going to wait for the next bus."

I started to walk off, but Keshawn grabbed my shoulder. "You going to leave me hanging like that? Just wait for me by the bus stop. I am going to Best Buy for a quick minute then I'll be right back."

Twenty minutes later, I saw Keshawn sprinting in my direction. Breathless, he was looking around nervously and his hat was soaked with perspiration. He had a Canon digital camera box with an extra memory card in his hands.

"Let's walk. This bus is taking too long."

I didn't feel like walking two miles to get home.

"Did you just steal that camera?"

He looked around and said, "Easy. Why are you talking so loud?"

"Just answer my question," I said, refusing to move any further.

"Are you the police or the feds? What I am *doing* is trying to get you out of trouble and get some money for my family, too."

He left me standing there, but I quickly caught up to him.

"How much did you pay for the camera?"

"I got it on sale."

"Sale, huh?" I said as I saw the devilish grin on his face.

"Yeah. My second cousin on Mom's side does inventory in the back of the store. He gave me the camera for *free*. I was going to get some more accessories, but I broke out when I heard someone coming into the storeroom."

"But why a camera?"

"Because I got the perfect come up. All I have to do is take some pictures of the bank around the way at opening and closing times for two days straight and get paid six hundred dollars."

"So how does this help me?"

"You live closer to the bank. And you can take the pictures then email them for me."

"Why can't you take the pictures and email them yourself?"

"I don't have a computer anymore," he said, looking down at the ground. "Yesterday, Mom had to sell it to help pay for the mortgage this month."

I wanted to say no, but when I saw him wiping tears from his eyes, I told him I was all in. I needed money, and I was not only helping him out, I was also assisting myself.

I woke up around 6:00 A.M., got ready, and made my way down the block. I walked on the other side of the street, avoiding Ms. Reynolds house. It was kind of chilly, so I put my hood over my head.

I made my way through the parking lot of Duane Reade, which was almost directly across the street from the bank. This was a great position for me because I could see who was entering the bank without being seen.

I didn't like waiting around like a sitting duck, but my black hoodie allowed me to blend in with the environment like a navy seal on a covert mission.

It was twenty minutes before I saw anyone.

A green Toyota Corolla with mismatched hubcaps pulled up, and out of the passenger side came a skinny black girl with a yellow shirt, black dress pants, and black high heels that made her look like an Amazon.

I took a picture.

Ten minutes later, I saw a security guard, who looked like the only thing he could guard was his plate, casually approach the glass doors. He was munching on a Twinkie, and some cream filling squirted on his shirt. He cursed loudly as he tried wiping off the mess with his other hand.

I took a picture.

Five minutes later, another employee, a black male with long cornrow braids, ugly green tie, and shiny steel-toed, brown wingtip shoes, approached the glass doors.

I took another snapshot.

I waited for another ten minutes to see if anyone else would show up. No one else did, so I made my way back to my house.

I got back inside at 6:59 A.M.

I quickly showered, got dressed, and met up with Keshawn, who was waiting patiently for me around the corner.

"Did you take the pictures?" He looked like he didn't get much sleep.

"No problems. It was a piece of cake."

"Cool. Don't forget to email them."

School was boring, as usual. When the last period bell rang, I met up with Keshawn, and we took the bus home. When I got inside, I went straight to my room and set my alarm clock for my next encounter with Lila.

I got up when my alarm rang; when I came outside, Keshawn was already sitting on my stoop. I told him to go to the backyard and get two brooms.

When he came back, we made a show of sweeping away in front of my house, appearing to be hard at work.

I looked over at Keshawn and smiled as Lila strolled down the block.

It was like she was floating on air. The sun seemed to be shining directly on her, making her glow like a angel with a halo. As soon as Lila got in front of my house Keshawn immediately dropped the broom, went up to her, and got a hug.

Standing there pissed off, I thought, *I was supposed to get the first hug.*

"Hi, Keke. You smell good. Do you have on cologne?" Lila asked.

Keshawn started blushing and shook his head. "No."

"Well, you smell good anyway."

It was my turn, and I walked up to Lila.

She rubbed my head, gave me a hug, and said, "You are so responsible, always cleaning up and all. I wish there were more people like you in the world. Anytime I see you guys, I just want to smile. Life isn't easy, especially for me, but you guys make me feel good. Both of you are like rays of sunshine, so pure and unfiltered."

Lila headed up the block, and Keshawn and I waited until we could no longer see her silhouette before we went our separate ways.

Granddad was in the kitchen, drinking a cup of coffee. "How's school treating you?"

"It's okay," I said, trying not to really engage him further.

"Good to hear. Good to hear. Did you wear that sweatshirt I bought you?"

Was he kidding? There was no way I would put that hideous thing on. Not even to sleep in. "Not yet, Granddad. I am saving it for a special occasion," I replied, not looking him directly in the eyes.

"I wanted to tell you that I am going on a little vacation. I'll be back in a couple of months. I always wanted to go to Europe, and I am going to be backpacking around like a teenager. I will write you when I can. I left you one of my prized possessions in your top drawer. Please take care of it for me."

I was in no mood to check on what he left me because Granddad didn't have anything that was of any value. He was too cheap and weird to possess anything I wanted.

"Sure," I said as I gave him a hug. "I'll guard it with my life."

I was relaxing on my bed when I heard knocking.

"Who is it?"

"It's me," Dennis answered.

I unlocked the door and let him in.

"Did you get the money yet? I don't want to get in trouble," he said, looking teary eyed.

"I'm working on it. I promise I won't let you down."

"Okay."

"Can I use your computer?"

"Sure."

Dennis' room had everything that I would kill for: a computer, an air conditioner, a mini-refrigerator, and a 32-GB IPod Touch hooked up to a BOSE stereo system, and he was about to get an IPhone next month if he maintained his straight A average.

I didn't understand why he needed a phone; his friends were seven, eight, and nine years old. What could they possibly be talking about that was of any importance?

I asked Dennis for some privacy. When he left, I quickly emailed the pictures to the address Keshawn gave me.

Just as I was about to shut down the computer, I heard the phone ringing. I went downstairs to the living room to get the cordless phone. I picked it up, and Keshawn was on the other end.

"It's almost closing time at the bank. Go take those pictures."

I put on my sneakers and hoodie and headed down the block and through the parking lot of Duane Reade. There were people coming in and out of cars and walking up and down the block. There was no way I would be able to take pictures without being seen.

That wouldn't have been a good situation for me. If someone had seen me and asked me what I had been doing, I would have been so nervous that I would have probably snitched on myself.

I headed across the street and around the corner facing the west side of the bank. I looked around and stood by a house that gave me a pretty good view of the bank. The house had a huge tree in the front yard and shrubs that were cascading over to the sidewalk. The house was dark inside, and no one was home from what I could tell.

I quickly jumped over the fence and camouflaged myself near the shrubs. I waiting until it was 7:20 P.M. I took a couple of snapshots as fifteen employees exited the bank at the same time. The security guard was the last one to come out, and he looked around before locking the doors.

I took another snapshot.

The security guard stood in front of the bank, munching on another Twinkie. When he was finished, he walked over to a brown, raggedy looking station wagon and drove off.

I took another snapshot.

I put the camera in my back pocket and waited until the coast was clear before jumping over the fence and making my way back home.

As I walked through the door, I saw Mama standing right in front of the refrigerator.

"Boy, where are you coming from?"

My head was so rattled, I didn't know what I was actually going to tell her. "I w...wasss..."

"Don't say another word. I am no mood to hear any fabricated stories tonight. Just go wash up, so we can have dinner."

As I washed my hands in the bathroom, I breathed a deep sigh of relief. Whew! I was almost busted.

Mama served up one of her specialty meals: fried chicken, potato salad, collard greens, macaroni and cheese, cornbread, and a tossed salad. She made us eat a salad with most meals, and I always drowned mine with French dressing because I didn't like vegetables. Especially cold ones.

I was in taste-bud heaven as I devoured the meal. I piled up my plate for seconds.

Mama looked worried when Dennis didn't follow suit. When she went to the kitchen to check on the dessert, I whispered, "Are you trying to get us busted? Act normal before Mama starts asking questions."

By the time Mama came back, Dennis had his plate piled up so high that food was dropping off the sides. That brought a big smile to her face.

After eating three large portions of apple pie with French vanilla ice cream and washing the dishes, I went straight to bed.

I woke up early and went down the block, my black hoodie covering my head. I went through the Duane-Reade parking lot and positioned myself to take pictures.

I began snapping pictures when I saw the same skinny black girl, who was wearing the same outfit she had on yesterday. Shortly afterwards, the security guard appeared, but this time he was eating a muffin, and I heard him curse when half of it fell on the floor as he tripped getting through the door.

I took a couple more snapshots.

The young guy with the braids had on another colorful ensemble, and I took some pictures again as he knocked on the glass door and the security guard let him in.

I got everything I needed and went back home.

I devoured three bowls of Frosted Flakes, and I was about to pour myself some orange juice when I heard my doorbell ring.

It was Keshawn. He finally used the doorbell. Something had to be wrong.

"Are you having an out of body experience?"

"Well, UFOs, abductions, and paranormal and spiritual case studies are all connected and…"

I should have known better than to open my mouth. "I am not in the mood for all that information. If you keep this up, I am not going to let you in."

Keshawn stopped talking, and I opened the door and let him in then took my bagel out of the toaster.

"What's good?" he said, as he watched me buttering my bagel.

As he came closer, a terrible smell overtook me. I looked around the kitchen, thinking that something was spoiled. I couldn't quite locate the smell, but something was definitely rancid.

"Do you smell that?" I asked Keshawn, who didn't seem perturbed by the smell.

"Uh-huh," he replied as he took in a couple deep breaths. "It takes you by surprise right."

He slowly raised his arms, and I almost passed out from the stench.

"Did you take a shower this morning?"

"I haven't showered for three days," he replied, with a smile on his face.

"Why not? You smell like a walking garbage can, and your funk is about to incinerate my nose hairs."

"Check this out," he said as he reached into his book bag. "I was reading this article that I found in one of my mother's magazines, talking about pheromones."

"Phero who?"

"Not phero who. Pheromones."

"What are phero-mones?"

Keshawn shook his head as if to say that I should know the answer to that. "Let me jog your memory, Einstein. We learned this in hygiene, first semester. Pheromones are a natural chemical that trigger a natural behavioral response in another member of the same species."

I was really trying to figure out where he was going with all this stuff and started scratching my head.

"I know, I know. I am talking another language again. So I'll break it down for you. See how Lila reacted to my smell the other day. She said that I smelled good, right?"

"Yeah. What's your point?"

"I didn't bathe that day. When I left my house in the morning, I just sprayed on some deodorant, which gave me a sweet and sour kind of scent," he explained, with his hands still raised above his head. "I've decided to take it a step farther. I'm not going to bathe or use any deodorant for the next week." He seemed excited as he continued rambling out information like a computer producing a spreadsheet. "Moths and butterflies release their pheromones into the air and attract a mate as far as six-point-two-five miles away. I am going to get mad girls today."

"You smell like a walking piece of doo-doo. You should go back home and shower."

He smiled. "Don't worry. I got everything under control. Just watch and learn."

We made our way to the bus stop. As Keshawn passed by a couple girls, they turned their heads, exclusively focusing on him.

"I know you see those girls checking me out," Keshawn said as he waved and blew a kiss in their direction. "Didn't I tell you this was going to happen?"

Keshawn should have taken another look.

What I saw was that one of the girls was looking at the bottom of her shoes like she just stepped in something, and her friend told her that the smell was coming from the boy who just passed and that they weren't getting on the same bus with him.

As the late bell rang, we made our way to our homeroom. I was practically holding my breath as I walked three steps behind Keshawn.

"What is the smell?" Mariah Morgan shouted.

Other student started looking around like they were trying to locate the horrible smell, as well.

"I don't know but whatever it is *stinks*. I think I am going to throw up," one of Mariah's friends said.

It was getting louder in the hallway, and with all that commotion, I lost sight of Keshawn.

When I located him, he was approaching a bunch of eighth-grade girls who were on the cheerleading team. They only fraternized with the basketball and football players and never spoke to us because we were classified as civilians (a.k.a. simple people with non-important lives).

"Ladies, how are you today?" he said as he raised his left hand and placed it in on the locker next to them so he could appear cool.

"*Yyuckk*. You smell something *terrible*." Penelope Cunningham, the captain of the cheerleading team, held her nostrils. "Get away from me and go take a bath."

Everyone started laughing, and Keshawn's face turned red.

I had to give it to him, he smoothly took his hand down off the locker and disappeared amongst the students who were scattering in the hallway, trying to get to their next class as the first bell rang.

I found Keshawn at the end of the hallway.

"How did that pheromone thing work out for you?" I asked, pinching my nostrils and imitating Penelope Cunningham.

He stared at me, and when I burst out laughing, he joined in.

"I hope you learned your lesson. Don't be coming to school smelling like roasted garlic, chopped onions, and five cups of yak piss," I said, still laughing.

"I am going to see if the nurse will let me shower in her office at lunchtime."

I nodded. "Good idea." I began pinching my nostrils like Penelope again.

As Christian approached us, we stopped laughing. "Yo, Keshawn, you got the rest of those pictures or what?"

I was stupefied.

I would never think in a zillion years Keshawn would have any dealings with Christian. Especially when he knew that Christian was the reason that I needed money in the first place.

"Yeah, I got you. You'll have everything by tomorrow."

As the late bell rang, Keshawn and I began walking to our next period class. I was still pissed.

"All of a sudden, you're doing deals with that fool. How could you betray me like that?"

"Look, don't be all proud. There is always pride before the fall. I need money, you need money."

I couldn't concentrate for the rest of the day. When eighth period was over, I met up with Keshawn, even though I wanted to tell him that boys didn't behave like that.

"I think my mother is losing it. She's been talking to herself, saying that she saw Matthew and that he wasn't really dead and she knows for a fact that he faked his death. And that my father was coming home soon and would go looking for Matthew and bring him back home to her."

Everyone in school knew that Keshawn's mother drank like it was going out of style, and I didn't want to tell him that it was the liquor talking for her.

When we got back around the way, Keshawn convinced me to take the last set of pictures and follow him to Christian's house to collect the money.

I had all the pictures taken at 7:20 P.M. and went back home and lay in bed for a while.

I snuck out at 8:00 P.M.

Christian lived in the back part of our neighborhood, and the houses were way bigger than the ones Keshawn and I lived in.

I didn't see any bottles, candy wrappers, loose papers, or dog doo-doo anywhere. It seemed like even the leaves on the trees were in perfect order.

I couldn't stop looking at Christian's lawn.

It was greener than green and looked as if someone painted it on, because they were no patches, weeds, or discoloration. Nothing was out of place.

Keshawn rang the doorbell, and I heard "London

Bridge Is Falling Down" chiming in the background.

We waited for about a minute before the door was opened. A tall, lanky dude with long boney arms, broad shoulders, light brown eyes, and reddish, unkempt hair stood in the doorway.

"How can I help you?" he growled in a surprisingly deep voice.

"We are here to see Christian," Keshawn answered.

He crossed his arms then began moving closer to Keshawn.

"What's your government?"

"My what?"

"Your name, shorty."

"Keshawn," he replied, with some base in his voice. "I didn't catch *your* name."

He looked at Keshawn and laughed.

"Because I didn't throw it. Shorty."

He motioned for us to come inside.

"Christian told me a lot about you and your boy. Let me see, your name is Penny, right?" He started laughing.

I didn't think that was funny and gave him a screw-face.

"Take it light, shorty. Your name is Brandon Stewart, right?"

I nodded.

He shut the door behind us. "Take off your sneakers and leave them by the door."

I felt stupid as I saw the big hole that showed off my big toe.

The house was spacious. As we walked along a long corridor, I looked down and marveled at how shiny the wooden floors were.

Mama would have definitely appreciated that.

We had to settle for cheap looking tiles because we couldn't afford wood floors.

Christian had a lot of stuff in his house: paintings that

looked expensive, sculptures on tiny pedestals, and a crystal chandelier that looked like it was imported.

We stopped at a huge open space that had to be the living room. There sat what appeared to be a seventy-five-inch plasma TV, enclosed inside the wall, with a BOSE surround sound system sitting like toy soldiers on little stands on the walls.

The bugged out thing about that was that I didn't see any wires coming from the TV or the speakers. I knew that cost a lot of money to do because everything had to be wired inside the walls.

The decor in the room was classy, as my mother would say. Black leather couches that still had that new smell were positioned in a big U shape. You could see the TV at every angle you looked. The drapes were gold to match the painted walls.

I looked at my feet as they practically sank into the plush black carpet.

Christian came into the living room, sporting blue basketball shorts with a matching blue sleeveless t-shirt. He instructed us to have a seat, and Keshawn and I plopped down on the couch, nestled comfortably like two birds in a nest.

I looked around, trying to locate any family portraits. I wanted to know where his parents were and what they did for a living, but I wasn't going to get all up in his business.

Christian said, "I see you guys met my brother, Marquis. Do you want something to drink?"

I didn't feel comfortable as Marquis stared at me like I was going to try to steal something.

"I'm good," I replied.

"I'll take a Sprite," Keshawn said, licking his lips. He was mad greedy.

He should have been focusing on getting the money and leaving.

Christian signaled for his brother to get the Sprite.

Marquis didn't take his eyes off us as he opened a cabinet and pulled out a bottle that looked like champagne.

"Young bucks, this is Cristal. It's usually three-fifty per bottle, but this bottle is worth a thousand. The earlier the year, the more it costs," he said as he unwrapped the gold foil on the top of the bottle, popped the cork then took a long swig. "What the rappers say, *balllinnnnn!*"

"You got the pictures?' Christian asked, looking at Keshawn, who looked at me.

"It's right here," I said as I took out the camera.

Christian got up and walked behind the couch, standing over my shoulder. "That's a good shot. You could be a professional," he said as he practically breathed down my neck.

Marquis came behind me and was peeking over my shoulder as well. "Perfect. That's everything I need," he said as he took another swig of the champagne, which was almost halfway empty.

Christian reached into his pocket and took out six crisp hundred dollar bills and handed them to Keshawn.

Keshawn's eyes opened wide as he saw the money.

I was getting up to leave but stopped as Marquis began talking.

"Keshawn, can I discuss something with you in private?"

Keshawn left the living room, and I felt uncomfortable sitting near Christian, the one person I hated more than anything else in the world.

"Do you want to play some video games?"

Christian turned my life topsy turvy, and now he was acting like we were cool. Was he on drugs? But rocking the boat could end up in disaster, especially since I didn't get my share of the money yet.

"What games you got?" I said, trying to act like everything was copasetic.

It was like a scene out of a James Bond movie.

Christian pushed a book on his bookshelf, which opened another, smaller cabinet door. He had Playstation 2, Playstation 3, WII, and the X-Box 360.

I told Christian to pop in *Tekken 3* for the Playstation 2.

I was having a good time kicking his butt. He kept restarting the game like that was going to help him. I was that nice in the game. He couldn't beat me with my eyes closed.

I looked at the clock and realized we were playing for over an hour. Christian pressed the reset button again. In my peripheral vision, I saw Keshawn wobble into the living room. I caught him when he almost landed on me as he stumbled in my direction.

"Keshawn, were you drinking?" I asked as I helped him to the couch.

"Just a little, but I'm good," he responded, slurring his words.

Marquis just laughed and went back to the cabinet and opened another bottle of champagne. The cork went flying up in the air and landed on the couch next to me. He took a swig and wiped his mouth before speaking. "Yo, Brandon. You want to make another three hundred dollars?"

Before I could say a word, Keshawn butted right in. "I'm down with that," he said, appearing to show no effects that he was drinking.

I guess talk of money miraculously made him sober up.

"So what I got to do?" Keshawn said, eagerly awaiting instructions.

"You don't have to do anything. He didn't ask you, he asked me." I said, staring at Keshawn. I wasn't going to let him give me thirty percent, or even fifty percent of the profits. I wanted one hundred percent of the profits.

"Chill, Keshawn. Who knew?" Marquis said, gulping down more champagne. "Your boy got some heart. I'll keep you in mind for the next time."

"I'm down like four flat tires on a car," I said, feeling good about the chance of making some more loot.

"I'm not really good with computers, so I want you to email the pictures to someone for me."

I thought, *That's all I have to do for three hundred dollars? This is as easy as counting one two three.* I followed Marquis to what looked like a den.

He pointed to the computer that was located at the corner of the room.

As I sat in front of the screen, I looked around the room and noticed the polished wood desk and, sitting on it, a pendulum that swung back and forth.

There were all kinds of books on the mahogany wood shelves, and I wondered who read them. The names looked foreign, and I knew none of them belonged to Christian because he never did any schoolwork. He just copied off someone else.

Most people looked at it as an honor for him to choose them to cheat off. Christian had it like that in school.

I put the memory stick in the printer and began sending the pictures to the email address he wrote down. I used Dennis' email address because I didn't have one, thanks to Mama, who said I couldn't get one until I brought up my "mediocre grades."

I had almost finished emailing the images when a cat jumped out from nowhere.

"You almost scared me half to death," I said as the cat brushed past my leg and disappeared to the other side of the room.

I was about to shut down the computer when the cat popped up out of nowhere again and was next to my leg.

I reached down to pet the cat, but, when my hand came close to its head, it ran off.

I got up and followed it as it headed inside a closet that was half open. I began opening the closet but it was stuck. I looked closer, and a pair of sneakers blocked the entrance. I bent down and began moving the sneakers.

I quickly kicked them back into the closet and ran back to the empty seat by the computer when I heard footsteps approaching the door.

"Everything good back here?" Marquis said as he entered.

"Everything is go...ood," I stuttered, not really giving him any eye contact.

"Just checking," he said as he handed me three hundred-dollar bills. Then he escorted me back to the living room.

Keshawn was snoring on the couch, so I shook him. "Yo, it's getting late. We should go home," I whispered in his ear.

He started to mumble something I couldn't quite make out as he closed his eyes. It wasn't too long before he was snoring again.

I looked over at Christian, who was focused on playing *Afro Samurai* for the Playstation 3.

"What's the hurry again?" Keshawn said as I started shaking him for the second time.

"My mother," I replied starting to raise my voice. "I got to go."

Christian put his game on pause. "It's getting late, anyway. You guys should roll out."

I was moving quickly up the block, and Keshawn was struggling to keep up.

"Slow down. You're acting like you just saw a ghost or something."

"I think Christian's brother was the one that robbed Pops' store and stabbed him."

"You are really bugging. How did you come up with that one? Are you drunk?"

"No, I'm not drunk. I didn't have a sip, remember?

And why would I say that if I didn't believe it."

Keshawn shrugged and walked away.

"I'm not bugging. I saw some white Chuck Taylors in a closet, and they looked like they had blood on them."

He started laughing. "That's all the evidence you got? Mad people are rocking Chuck Taylors. That's the new style."

"Yo, I'm serious," I said, pleading my case. "I bet you anything it was Christian's brother."

"You are definitely bugging," he said as he began laughing again. "The guy who held up the store was shorter than Marquis."

"No, he wasn't."

"How you know?"

"If anyone should know, it would be me."

"What makes you an expert on height, all of a sudden?"

"Because he had me by my throat. Remember? Or did you forget?"

"How does that money feel in your pocket?" he asked as he counted his portion out loud.

"It feels fine," I said, rubbing my fingers against the money.

"Good. That's all that counts."

"I bet Marquis is going to rob the bank around the way."

"I just made three hundred dollars, and you made six hundred. That money will help both our situations. Or have you forgotten? Keep your eyes on the finish line," he replied. "What Christian and his brother do is their problem. Not ours."

He picked up the pace in the middle of the block, and I hurried to catch up to him. He was real quiet as I walked beside him. He acted like I wasn't even there. I hated when he was silent, but I knew it meant he was really agitated.

I tried striking up a conversation. "Keshawn, I just heard a cricket chirp, and maybe if we listened we could calculate the temperature outside."

Keshawn ignored me and began walking even faster.

I started feeling guilty that I brought up the subject about Christian's brother in the first place.

We were a block away from my house when he started talking to me. "Do you remember last summer?"

I nodded. "How could I ever forget?"

On a humid Friday night in July, Keshawn and I were sitting on my steps, just hanging out. I wanted to get some Italian ices from the store.

"Just chill. I am picking up a bad vibe tonight," Keshawn said.

"What are you, a psychic?" I replied. "I'll be back."

I got up to go, but he grabbed me by my shoulder.

"If you move another step, I am going to tell your parents that you were the one that broke Ms. Reynolds living room window with a wiffle ball."

I quickly sat back down. I didn't need the drama. Even though Ms. Reynolds told them she saw me running inside when it happened, they believed me. I never lied to them before, and she had no proof.

Luckily for me, the truth wasn't revealed.

I would have been on double punishment.

I was surprised to hear on the news the day after that the store, which is now closed, was shot up and three people were killed around 10:30 P.M.

That would have been the exact same time I would have been walking into the store.

Keshawn saved my life that day, and I would forever be in his debt.

Mama must be working late again, because I didn't see her car in the driveway. I went straight to my room. When

I looked down on the floor, I saw little crumbs by my bed. It had to be Dennis. I was in no mood to deal with him, so I just quickly got undressed and hopped into bed.

It was hard for me to fall asleep, and I got up and went to the bathroom to splash some water on my face.

I came back to a hot room and opened my window, hoping to let some air in. It wasn't working. I took off my undershirt and relaxed in my bed with my favorite hulk underwear on. I stared at the crack in my ceiling because I was restless.

Marquis was on my mind. He looked, spoke, and acted like a shady individual, and I couldn't understand why Keshawn didn't see it.

I got up and searched for the money in my pants.

Keshawn was right. The money did feel good in my hands, and I shouldn't think so much about Marquis, because what he did really wasn't my problem.

I looked at the crack in my ceiling again and wondered what state my dad was in.

I was awakened when a rock hit my window.

I yelled at Keshawn then told him I would be down in about thirty minutes.

I went to the bathroom, and Dennis was already inside brushing his teeth. He looked tired.

"What's up, bro? Did you get the money yet? We only have a week left," he said before gargling with mouthwash.

"I got six hundred dollars, and I am working on the rest."

"I knew you could do it. I knew it. You are the best big brother in the world," he said as he hugged me so hard that I didn't think he was going to let me go.

I rubbed him on his head.

The idea that he believed in me made me feel good.

I quickly showered and didn't even care what clothes I picked out to wear. I didn't feel like going to school. All I wanted to do was get right back into bed.

I came downstairs, and Keshawn was waiting on my stoop.

"Man, you take forever in the morning."

It was a nice day, and I laughed to myself, noticing that he still had that stupid hat on.

"You should have seen my mom's face when she found money in one of her old bags," he said as he adjusted his hat.

"Didn't she know that you put it there?"

"Mom's been so stressed, she wouldn't care if the tooth fairy put it under her pillow," he said, looking down at the ground. "She still hasn't found a job yet. The recession sucks."

I didn't feel like taking the long way, so we quickly walked up the block, avoiding Ms. Reynolds house.

When we reached the corner, I saw a cop car roaring down the street. It wasn't even five seconds before I saw another three cop cars zoom past, almost hitting a pedestrian who had the right of way.

Keshawn and I watched intensely, trying to figure out where they were going in such a hurry, so early in the morning. There were a couple of adults standing by the bus stop watching the action.

The cop cars screeched in front of the bank, and I looked at Keshawn as if to say, "I told you so."

We walked towards the bank, trying to get as close as possible.

I saw two officers jump out of each of the three police cars. Four officers looked at each other, made some kind of hand signals then cautiously opened the doors of the bank, with their weapons drawn.

A fourth squad car pulled up and had the traffic blocked in both directions on Merrick Boulevard.

An overweight police officer who was standing on the corner squeezed into his squad car and began talking on his walkie-talkie.

He looked annoyed as he came back out and took out some yellow caution tape. He and another officer, a skinny black lady who looked like a teenager, quickly had the area completely sealed off.

I wondered if someone got shot, and Keshawn and I both looked to see what was going to happen next.

"What do you think just happened?" an old lady asked another elderly man who was standing right next to us.

Twenty minutes later, the officers were still inside, and we still didn't have a clue as to what was going on in the bank.

A bigger crowd formed across the street, and everyone

had their own ideas about what was going on.

An old man with a strange looking cane said, "I think someone triggered the silent alarm by mistake."

"The security guard probably had a heart attack because of all that weight he's carrying," a lady who had on a dress that was way too tight said.

"I think someone got shot," a man who had this ugly green tie on said.

"I bet you someone robbed the bank," the old lady who was standing beside us said.

I looked over to Keshawn and whispered, "I told you that Christian's brother was going to rob the bank."

"You're just as bad as everyone else," he said, shaking his head. "Who told you that the bank got robbed? It could be a false alarm. Don't go jumping to any conclusions. Besides, I don't see how this is our business, anyway."

We waited another fifteen minutes before Keshawn got annoyed. "I'm bouncing. There is nothing to see. You can wait around and waste time, if you like."

I looked at my watch and realized he was right. We had wasted far too much time just standing around for nothing.

"It's a nice day. Let's walk to school," Keshawn said, looking up at the sky.

As we began walking down the block, I heard a cell phone ringing. I looked around to see where it was coming from. Keshawn rummaged through his book bag, pulled out a cell phone, and answered it.

I didn't know he had a cell phone, and it looked like the new Blackberry.

I eavesdropped on his conversation.

"Uh-ummm, uh-ummmm, okay, okay. All right, we will meet you guys in about twenty minutes."

"What's going on?" I asked.

Keshawn was cryptic. "I was just presented with a unique opportunity that would make us a couple thousand in a few hours and possibly ten thousand by the end of the week."

"I am not taking any pictures, nor am I selling anything else," I replied, crossing my arms.

"I feel you. They are about to cut off the electricity and the water and the gas, and the cable got turned off yesterday," he said, playing with the cell phone. "I was assured that it would be like taking away candy from a baby. And it's completely undetectable and untraceable. All we need to do is…"

Keshawn stopped in mid sentence and began humming that stupid song from Pops' store.

"Come on man, spill the beans."

"Just trust me. I'll explain everything when I get all the details."

We made an about face and passed the bank again. Nothing was happening, and the crowd across from the bank was larger.

"Where are we going?" I asked as we continued walking up the block.

"First to your house, so you can get all the money that you made yesterday."

"For what?"

"Trust me. I'll explain everything to you later."

I snuck into my house, grabbed the money that I stashed in my underwear draw, and tiptoed back downstairs and out the door without disturbing Dennis.

We walked back up the block; when we went past the bank, everything was back to normal. The yellow tape was gone, the cop cars were gone, and I saw people going in and out of the bank like nothing happened.

We walked about sixteen blocks to an underpass where the Long Island Railroad stopped. Keshawn began looking around, and I heard his cell phone ringing again.

"Hello—I see the car."

We slowly approached a black sedan with tinted windows and black and chrome rims. I didn't know what kind of car it was. The only time I saw something like that was on *MTV Cribs*.

"That's a Maserati," Keshawn said, identifying the car for me. He knew a lot about cars. His father used to be a top mechanic in a luxury dealership in Manhattan before he got hooked on drugs.

We approached the rear passenger door, and I heard a click.

As we entered, I could detect that distinctive new car smell. I felt like I landed on a cloud as I sat on the supple leather seats. I looked to the front of the car and saw two familiar faces. Marquis was in the driver's seat, and Christian was riding shotgun. Marquis was eyeballing me through the rearview mirror.

"Ya'll ready to get some money?" Christian said, giving his brother a high five.

Keshawn yelled, "Let's get *pzzzzaid*."

Marquis turned on the air conditioner, and, in just a few seconds, I felt like I was in Antarctica.

I wanted to tell him to turn it down as goose pimples were popping up all over my skin, but I didn't want to look like a punk. I began shaking my legs, trying to warm myself up.

Marquis was fidgeting with the navigation system like he never used it before; after twenty minutes, I heard the car say, "Turn left in one hundred yards."

It was a pretty quiet ride, and Marquis paid Keshawn no mind when he asked if he could turn on the radio.

It got colder as he turned up the AC.

Keshawn didn't seem to mind. That wool hat on his head was finally coming in handy, and I wished I had one on, too.

Even though I was shivering, it felt really good to be in such a high end luxury car with all the imaginable amenities.

We jumped on the highway, and the car roared like a hungry mountain lion. Other drivers on the road were breaking their necks trying to see who was inside. I felt like a celebrity. Marquis was driving at a hundred miles an hour, but I didn't notice until Keshawn said that it felt like we were only going fifty.

"That's one of the many perks of having an over a hundred thousand dollar foreign car. They always possess technology to the tenth degree," Keshawn explained.

That was the total opposite of Mama's car. After she took our Monte Carlo past fifty-five miles per hour, it showed its disapproval by shaking like a strung out drug addict.

We got off the highway and came around a bend that said ramp speed twenty-five miles an hour. Marquis was still doing forty miles per hour and cleared that bend like we were on a straightaway.

As I looked through the window, I noticed we were not in the nicest of neighborhoods; the sun seemed to be hiding from everyone. I didn't blame it. We were definitely in the "hood." As we stopped at a light, an older man who looked like he hadn't bathed in days tried washing the windshield.

"I hate bums," Marquis yelled as he ran a red light and almost hit the man, who jumped out of the way.

We drove another couple blocks, past several apartment buildings.

I whispered in Keshawn's ear. "Where are we?"

"The projects. Baisely Projects, to be exact. My mother used to live here when she was younger."

I wasn't too familiar with the projects because no one I knew lived there, but, by looking at some of the people in the streets, you definitely had to know how to protect yourself.

I saw two teenagers around my age running down the street with a case of beer in their hands. Marquis noticed them and lowered his window. "Put that work in. Get that money, young 'uns."

They didn't even look back to see who was talking but cut up a block and into a park.

We were parking when I noticed that you could see the car behind us on the navigation screen.

Keshawn yelled, "A rear camera. That is sick."

Everyone got out, and I saw two kids who could be no older than me riding bikes that were way too small for them. They were ice-grilling us like we owed them money as they pedaled toward us.

Marquis popped the trunk, grabbed a book bag, and put it on his shoulder like a kindergartener coming home from school.

One of the boys stopped in front of the car. "Yo, that whip is serious. How much you pay for it?"

Marquis chuckled. "If you got to ask then it's out of your price range."

The boy gave Marquis a cold look that said, if he thought he had a chance, he would just jack him for his car.

Marquis seemed to sense that he had offended the boy. "Just playing, shorty. Tell your man to come over here, I got something for the both of you."

The boy whistled, and his friend quickly pedaled over to us.

Marquis reached into his pocket and pulled out two hundred-dollar bills. "Make sure no one sits on my car. And if you do a good job, I'll give you another two hundred when I come back."

"Bet. We'll guard your car with our lives," they both said as they quickly put the money in their pockets and stood in front of the car with their arms crossed, taking turns looking in all directions.

We walked through the courtyard, and you could see kids running up and down.

I heard a lot about the projects, and I didn't know how I should act. Marquis and Christian seemed comfortable in this environment. I was scared to death and walked closely to Keshawn as I looked around cautiously.

In the distance, you could see a bunch of guys on a bench, drinking beer, smoking cigarettes, and talking loudly. We were getting closer to the group of men. A muscular guy who had long dreads and appeared to be in his early twenties was the first one to spot us coming in their direction. He stood up and began walking toward us, and his crew got up and walked closely behind him.

"Yo, Marquis, what's up?" he yelled, looking in our direction.

"What up, E Money? Why you screaming out my government?" Marquis said as he acted like he was going to his waist for a weapon. "I may have to kill you now."

E Money was right in front of us and gave Marquis a bear hug like he hadn't seen him in years.

The only thing on my mind was how he got the nickname E Money. No one around there looked rich at all.

"You ready to take care of business?" Marquis asked.

"No doubt," E Money said, staring long and hard at Christian. "Is that little Christian? You got mad big."

"I've been eating my Wheaties."

Christian laughed then gave E Money a bear hug, too.

"Yo, Marquis, who them?" E Money asked, not taking his eyes off me and Keshawn.

"Don't worry. They Christian's boys."

"I hope they're not working for the Feds, because me and jail don't mix. Like a fat girl wearing a two-piece bikini, it's just not a good look," E Money said.

Marquis laughed. "They good. Don't worry. Let's go back to your crib to take care of business."

E Money was still looking us up and down and made a comment to Marquis about Keshawn wearing a ski hat in this warm weather.

All the buildings looked the same, and I was trying to pay attention to where we were going, but it was like a big maze.

We got to a building and went through the first set of doors. I got worried when I saw some bullet holes, and I hoped that no one would be shooting today.

E Money buzzed apartment 6D. I heard a lady's voice answer.

"It's me, Grandma," E Money announced.

I heard another buzz, and we went through the second set of steel doors. I could smell urine, and I wondered why someone would pee inside the building. The elevator wasn't working, and we walked up the dark staircases to the sixth floor.

We waited outside the apartment as I heard someone fidgeting with the locks before the door opened.

"Come give Grandma a hug." The lady embraced E Money while rocking him from side to side.

This is his grandmother? I thought. She could easily pass for his sister or even his girlfriend.

She had on a tight pair of True Religion jeans, Dolce & Gabanna t-shirt, Prada shoes, Gucci watch, and a Louis Vuitton belt.

She looked past E Money, who she called Ernest, and kept her gaze on the rest of us. "I hope you boys aren't going to do any funny stuff up in here."

"Come on, Grandma. You know me better than that."

"I do, so that is why I am giving you a warning. I don't want no cops kicking down my door," she said, lighting a cigarette. "I had to replace one last week when they arrested your cousin. Remember?"

We walked into the living room, and I was surprised how elegantly it was decorated: white carpet with matching drapes, plasma TV, and white leather couches.

Christian, Marquis, and E Money went to the back of

the apartment while Keshawn and I sat on the couch with
E Money's grandma, who told us to call her Tweetie.

She left the living room momentarily and came back
with two Sprites.

I took a long sip and went to rest the can on the table
when Tweetie stopped me.

"Don't you see that coaster? Use it. Don't be messing
up anything in here."

I looked at Keshawn, and he was trying to hold in his
laughter.

Tweetie turned on the TV. "I love me some Jerry
Springer," she said as she cranked up the volume. "I mean,
I really, really, love me some Jerry Springer. Kick his butt,
girl. I can smell a liar like a hound dog. He is trifling. Lying
about he never saw that woman before."

Granddad would say she was acting really ghetto, and
he would be right. Tweetie was talking to the TV like they
could actually hear her. Me and Keshawn were trying not
to laugh.

About half an hour later, Christian came to the living
room and told us to join him in the back.

E Money's room was surprisingly immaculate. His bed
was neatly made, and he had several posters of Michael
Jordan and one of Albert Einstein, Martin Luther King,
and Robert Kennedy, Jr. He also had a desktop computer,
three laptops, and two expensive looking inkjet printers.
Everything looked brand new.

That was not what I expected from E Money.

He looked like a thug, talked like a thug, walked like a
thug, but, by looking at the books that were strategically
placed all over his room on polished wooden bookshelves,
I knew he was very intelligent.

"You got the money?" Christian asked Keshawn.

Keshawn looked at me, and I pointed to my left pocket.

"Me first," Marquis said, taking the book bag off his
shoulders and carefully opening it. He pulled out a stack of

money that had a paper band around it.

That was weird, because the only time I could remember seeing that kind of band was when I was in the bank. The tellers would pull them out when they had just got some new money.

I wanted a clearer look to confirm my suspicions, but I was blocked by Marquis' wide shoulders.

Marquis took out another banded stack of money and put it on the floor next to E Money. He went in and out of the bag about eight more times before he stopped.

E Money got excited.

"I likes that. How much money you working with?"

"Ten stacks. I like working with even numbers."

I looked at Keshawn, confused.

"That means ten thousand dollars," he whispered.

I badly wanted to get a closer look at the money; maybe I could recognize a bank seal or something.

I tried positioning myself closer to Marquis, but now I was blocked by Christian's broad shoulders. I guessed that trait ran in the family.

"That's a lot of cheese. Did you rob a bank or something?" E Money said, playing with the money.

I looked over to Keshawn, shooting him a look as if to say I told you so.

"And so what if I did," Marquis replied with a devilish grin. "So how much can you get me?"

"A hundred and fifty percent mark-up on everything you give me. But I am going to need more time to satisfy your request. You didn't tell me you were rolling like that."

I still didn't know what they were selling or buying, and I wondered if I was caught up in some kind of drug deal. I was never around drugs before. The closest I came was from watching TV.

I started looking around the room for evidence. I spotted a microwave and a spoon. Did they use that to make the drugs? I was getting confused. Or was that baking soda with a pot, needles, and small plastic bags?

I continued scanning the room. E Money had a medium-sized Sponge Bob lying on the other side of the room. There was no way that he would watch Sponge Bob, let alone buy a stuffed toy. It didn't seem feasible.

I wondered if it was a hidden camera that he set up to reduce his sentence because he was already busted by the cops. Or maybe Tweetie and her partners were going to be crashing through the door any minute and arresting us and locking us up for the rest of our lives.

I continued looking around the room, hoping it wasn't an undercover sting.

My palms were getting sweaty. I started shaking my leg, trying to calm myself down. It wasn't working. I began feeling claustrophobic. I had to find a way to get out of there. I made up my mind that I wasn't going down for something I wasn't privy to beforehand.

"E Money, can I use the bathroom?"

"It doesn't work. Hold it in until I'm finished."

"I got to go real badly," I lied, fidgeting in place and holding my stomach. "I feel like I am about to bust."

E Money went into his closet and tossed me an empty water bottle. "Use that. But do it in the corner of the room, and don't let one drop of pee hit my carpet."

I wondered what Keshawn was thinking. When we locked eyes, he gave me a look that said I was spoiling everything.

I forced myself to pee in the bottle.

"Give me the money. We don't have all day," Christian said, looking at Keshawn.

Keshawn looked at me, and at first I didn't do anything. I just stared at him, trying to communicate with my eyes. I was telling him that we should leave right away.

He didn't get it. "Snap out of it. Give me the money."

I had no choice but to reach into my pocket as everyone in the room began looking at me suspiciously. I handed the money to Keshawn, and he gave it to E Money.

"Thank you. That will be a hundred and fifty percent mark-up for you guys, too."

I wondered what was going to happen next.

E Money went to his desktop computer and turned on the hard drive. There was space on the bed, so I sat in between Marquis and Christian to get a closer look.

"This is where all the magic happens," E Money said as he rubbed his hands together then cracked his knuckles.

E Money took a hundred dollar bill from one of the stacks Marquis gave him and put it on the scanner. He waited patiently as the image was scanned and showed up on his monitor. "I'm going to save this and open it up in Photoshop."

We all watched as E Money removed scratches and imperfections from the scanned image. Then he went over the image with his mouse, and—abracadabra—the serial numbers seemed to mysteriously change. He was right, it was just like magic.

"Your computer skills are off the hook. How much do I get again?" Marquis asked excitedly.

"As promised, a hundred and fifty percent return. Making it a grand total of twenty thousand five hundred—"

Keshawn interrupted. "I do believe that's twelve hundred fifty for us, right?"

"Yes, sir," E Money said, still playing with the image. "I'll work on yours first since you guys are getting back a smaller amount. I will need for you to go to the store and pick up a few products. The quicker you return, the faster I can work on your money."

E Money threw a hundred dollar bill at Keshawn, who gracefully caught it in mid-air.

Christian looked at me. "Go with Keshawn. We got some other business to take care of."

Keshawn and I walked past the living room, where we saw Tweetie fast asleep on the couch with a cigarette in her hand. I carefully removed it because I didn't want her to burn down the apartment, especially being that our money was inside.

When we reached the hallway, I took in a deep breath. I was kind of glad to be out of the apartment and even happier that it wasn't a sting operation.

Keshawn was practically jumping up and down in one spot. "This is the best hustle ever. You hear? The best. Instead of trying to find ways to get money, why not have someone make it for us? This is ingenious. I should have thought of it myself."

By the expression on my face, Keshawn knew that I wasn't too comfortable with everything. I calmed down when he reminded me that I didn't have much time left to replace Dennis' cello.

As we walked down the staircase, an old lady came out of nowhere. I jumped back.

"What you so jumpy for?" she yelled, holding her purse. "I should be the jumpy one. You kids today don't know how to work for anything. But you sure know how to *take, take, take.* You need to *wake up.* You are sleeping on the job of life. I remember a time when opportunity came knocking only once, and if you didn't open the door...well, you might as well kiss your butt goodbye."

It was like she had that speech memorized before she even saw us. She reminded me of Granddad, Mama, Mr. Rogers, and Ms. Reynolds all rolled up in one.

We ignored her and continued walking down the staircase.

When we got outside, E Money's friends were still sitting on the bench. When they saw us, they just nodded in our direction and quickly went back to their dice game.

"You know we got a pass, right?" Keshawn said.

"A pass? What kind of pass?" I asked incredulously.

"In the hood, if they know you aren't from around there and they see you looking out of place, they consider you 'bait.' You hope they just chase you, but you can get robbed, beaten up, and, the worst case scenario, killed. But by getting a pass, we kind of have a roam freely card that doesn't at least get revoked for the day."

We kept walking towards where we came in and saw the two boys standing by Marquis' car, protecting it like professional bodyguards.

"See, nobody touched the car," the taller one said. "Where the rest of your boys at?"

"They still taking care of business. They'll be down soon," Keshawn replied.

"We still going to get the rest of that money, right?" the shorter boy inquired.

Keshawn and I continued up the block. He turned around when this guy about my dad's age shouted, "Aren't you Claire's boy?"

Keshawn hesitantly replied, "Yeah."

"Let me holla at you for a minute," he said as he motioned to Keshawn to come closer.

I stood around idly as they chitchatted for about ten minutes. Keshawn made his way back over to me and began telling me who that stranger was.

He had gone to high school with Keshawn's mother and had fallen on some hard times and wanted to borrow some money.

We continued walking as the man yelled, "That's how it is. Your mother always thought she was uppity, and I remember when she used to bring you around here. Now you guys live in a house and all, but trust me, you'll be back. Right back in the projects with the rest of us where you *belong*."

Keshawn looked disgusted, and we picked up the pace as we walked up the block.

"People like that remind me how much I don't miss the projects at all, and that's why I can't afford to fail at getting this money. If I don't get all that I need then they'll be foreclosing on our house, and that would mean I'd be right back in the projects again."

We walked a couple of blocks before stopping at a rinky-dink auto store. Keshawn asked the clerk for some auto degreaser. He didn't know what brand to get, and he told the clerk to give him the best one he had.

Our next stop was a block away at this broke down looking Bodega. We walked inside, and I was surprised how clean it was as compared to the outside.

Keshawn got some no-name household cleaner spray, five toothbrushes, and four large plastic Tupperware bowls.

"What we need all this stuff for?" I asked as we made our way back to E Money's apartment building.

"I am not sure. But it has to be what you use to make the counterfeit money."

Tweetie was still sleeping, and we made our way to E Money's room. Keshawn gave E Money the bags full of the stuff we purchased. He dispensed everything onto his desk and got straight down to business.

I looked intently as he operated like a seasoned surgeon.

E Money took a five dollar bill and put it in the Tupperware bowl that he filled with auto degreaser. He soaked the money for about thirty seconds, took it out, and began brushing the money slowly back and forth with a toothbrush, like he was applying barbecue sauce on some pork ribs.

Then, he sprayed household cleaner on the five dollar bill until all the writing, images, and background disappeared on both sides.

I kept staring intently, because this was better than any magic trick I ever saw.

Next, E Money turned on a bright fluorescent lamp near his computer and began inspecting the money. It was completely clear except for the image of Abraham Lincoln that you could still see on the upper right corner.

I was amazed at how meticulous E Money's workmanship was.

Then, E Money went into his closet, took out a blow dryer, and dried the money for about twenty seconds. Afterwards, he put the money in the microwave for about a minute. Next, he took the money out of the microwave, went back to his computer, printed out the back and front image of a hundred dollar bill, and carefully cut it with a pair of scissors he had lying on his desk. He took some glue and posted both the front and back images of the hundred dollar bill directly on the original five dollar bill.

E Money passed the bill around so we could all get a better look. "Fellows, behold the masterpiece," he said, raising his hands like he was a prophet. He was grinning from ear to ear as we all stared at the money in adoration.

"This is absolutely beautiful," Christian said as he handed the money to Marquis a second time.

E Money told everyone to go back into the living room because he wanted to fully concentrate on his work so he didn't make any stupid mistakes.

Tweetie was still sleeping, and her obnoxious snore reminded me of Mama's car backfiring down the block.

Marquis looked tired. Before you knew it, he and Christian were sleeping like babies.

Something must be circulating in the air, because I felt Keshawn shaking me to get up.

I wiped some slobber off the side of my mouth as I got off the couch. We all went back to E Money's room. He was shutting down his computer.

"I'm done with the twelve hundred fifty dollars," he said, looking at me and Keshawn.

E Money passed a ten dollar bill to Keshawn, who inspected it and passed it to me.

I was looking for any visible defects. It looked and felt

real. I inspected it a second time.

Keshawn passed me some other bills. After inspecting them, I noticed that not all the money had Abraham Lincoln's image on the upper right hand corner.

I brought it to E Money's attention.

"Good catch, shorty," E Money said as I handed him back the money. "Each bill I did doesn't have the seal, so don't spend all the money in one place."

Keshawn looked at me as if to ask why I always spoiled things.

"These are the rules you need to follow," E Money said as he played with the scissors on his desk. "Try to purchase or pay stuff with a ones, fives, tens, or twenties. And be careful with the hundred dollar bills. I only gave you two hundred-dollar bills because they are the hardest ones to pass off. Actually, you may not want to use them because people are always inspecting those."

"Is there anything else we should know?" Keshawn said, hanging on every word like he was studying for an entrance exam.

"Let's say you want something to eat; go to a diner. Diners are the best place to use the money because you can usually put the money on the table then leave the establishment."

"Anything else we should do?" Keshawn inquired.

"Buy a lot of flowers with the money, preferably using twenties."

"I don't have a girlfriend. And I'm allergic to most flowers."

"It's not about girls or your allergies. It's about you getting rid of the fake money," E Money said as he laughed. "Peep this. On Jamaica Avenue, there are a bunch of people who are on the corners selling flowers. They are on the streets like roaches. Give them a twenty and buy either a five dollar or ten dollar bouquet. That way you'll get some change back and have real money in your possession that you can keep without worrying about getting busted with the counterfeit money. You can do this all day, every day in Brooklyn, Queens, Manhattan, Jersey, Bronx, Staten Island, and Long Island."

Christian turned to E Money. "So when them hundreds going to be ready?"

"Give me about twenty-four hours."

I let curiosity get the best of me. "Marquis, how are you going to pass off hundred dollar bills?"

"You guys are tadpoles, and Christian and I are great white sharks," Marquis said as he cracked a smile. "I could put you up on game. Do you have ten stacks?"

The idea of flipping ten stacks to $20,500 was definitely alluring, but Keshawn and I both said, "No."

"See me when you get your weight up."

We all left E Money's apartment and quickly walked down the stairs and out of the building. It was totally dark outside, and we made our way through the courtyard to Marquis' car.

The two boys were still on guard and looked happy when Marquis handed them another two hundred. They rode off in the darkness without even saying thank you.

Marquis popped the trunk and grabbed another book bag, and I wondered what was inside. Keshawn and I went to the back door, expecting Marquis to open up the car. He didn't.

"Yo, I feel like taking the bus home," he said, looking at Christian.

Keshawn looked at me, and, before we could comment, Christian and Marquis blended with the darkness as they walked up the block.

Keshawn pulled out his cell phone and called a cab. As luck would have it, the cab arrived in ten minutes, which Keshawn told me never happened in the hood. The ride was quick, and the cab driver kept looking in the rearview mirror, studying our faces. I figured he didn't trust us and wanted to be able to identify us if we tried to jump out of his cab without paying.

When we pulled up in front of my house, the cab driver made sure not to open the door until we handed him the money.

"That will be thirty dollars," he said forcefully.

Keshawn handed him two twenties through the Plexiglas, and the cab driver looked delighted when he told him to keep the change.

It was 9:30 P.M. when I got inside, and I was happy to see the note that Mama left saying she was working late again.

Dennis was probably waiting up, because as soon as I opened my door, he came rushing out of his room.

"Did you get the money?"

"Not all of it, but I have a good amount," I said as I gave him forty dollars.

"Should I save this just in case you need it later on?"

"Nah. I'm good. I got things under control."

Dennis hugged me so tightly that I almost fell backwards. After listening to him talk about how much of a great brother I was, I escorted him out.

I woke up as I heard a rock hit my window. Keshawn was really bugging. If he didn't watch it, he was going to break my window. I immediately got up, opened my window halfway, pulled up my blinds, and shouted at him.

"You need to stop acting like a caveman. When will you get it through your thick skull that—"

I stopped talking instantaneously when I saw Carol Whitaker standing there, straining her neck upwards.

I felt like such a geek in my Captain America pajamas, but I could tell Carol didn't notice them because she was still smiling at me.

"Hey, Carol. What's up?" I calmly asked, sticking my head out and not letting her see my shoulders.

Carol was dressed all in white: a miniskirt that stopped right above her knees, Lacoste shirt and sandals, even her fingernail and toenail polish. Her hair was pulled back in a ponytail, and her lip gloss was applied perfectly, making her lips extremely kissable.

I was taken aback when I noticed she was standing next to Penelope Cunningham, the leader of the cheerleading team and the one who dissed Keshawn the other day.

"Hi, Brandon. Hurry up and come downstairs," Carol's sweet voice echoed.

I think that was the fastest I ever showered in my life. I spent most of my time trying to figure out what I was going to wear.

I decided on the newest pieces of clothes I owned. Last year, Mama purchased me a pair of blue denim Sean John shorts with a black Sean John t-shirt, and this was the special occasion I was hoping for to unleash my outfit.

I didn't like that my sneakers were so dirty, but there

was nothing I could do about that. I just laced them up and quickly headed downstairs.

When I came outside, Keshawn, Penelope, and Carol were conversing on my stoop. As soon as Carol spotted me, she jumped off the stoop, ran up to me, and hugged me tightly. Her perfume was so intoxicating, I didn't want the moment to end, and I embraced her like I just came home from being in Iraq.

"Thank you so much for the Chanel earrings. They just came out," she said, playing with them in her ears.

I had no idea what she was talking about and looked over to Keshawn for an answer. He just winked, and I reminded myself that I would have to thank him later.

"It was nothing. I just wanted to give you a little something. An extraordinary girl like you always deserves the best," I said, playing it off.

"You are so sweet," she said, batting her eyelashes. "I've decided that I am going to the prom with you and not Christian. That's if you will still take me."

As I told her yes, I wondered if she could see how happy I was feeling inside.

Keshawn stood up and cleared his throat like he had an important announcement to make. "Dear friends, I have decided that we should not waste such a beautiful day being in school. I propose we go to the mall, get something to eat then do some shopping."

Penelope and Carol clapped like first graders during snack time.

I was in heaven as Carol sat on my lap, and Keshawn had his arms around Penelope. He whispered in her ear as she giggled.

A white Mercedes-Benz limo came down my block and stopped in front of my house. The driver slowly let down the passenger window.

Keshawn jumped up. "Let us depart. Our chariot awaits."

As we got inside, I saw a mini refrigerator, and we sat on the comfortable leather seats. You could easily fit ten people inside. Four Sprites were already opened, and we drank and giggled as we drove along.

I was so happy that I was around Carol and kept staring into her eyes as I had my arm around her waist. I owed Keshawn big time.

Thirty-five minutes later, we arrived at Roosevelt Field Mall in Long Island. That was the first time I was ever there. This place was way better than Jamaica Ave and Green Acres Mall put together.

"Nordstroms, Macy's, Bloomingdales, Armani, Coach...what more could a girl ask for?" Carol said as she looked at the directory of stores.

The first thing we did was get something to eat. Penelope and Carol ordered the same thing: scrambled eggs hard, sausage, bacon, and pancakes with maple syrup. I had an omelet with the works, and Keshawn had French toast, two fried eggs sunny side up, bacon, and sausage.

Carol and Penelope were completely relaxed as they got a manicure and a pedicure. Carol's feet looked so smooth I could eat off them. The lady who worked on them said that it was such a pleasure and that if all her customers took care of their feet like her they would be out of business.

Keshawn paid for everything, and I think the store owner was so happy to see a fifty-dollar tip he didn't even check the money.

We went into the Coach store on the second floor, and I bought Carol a pair of fancy looking loafers that cost $188. I paid in all twenties, and Keshawn was asking the salesclerk so many questions that she just put the money in the cash register and handed me the change.

Keshawn and I utilized the same philosophy we discussed in the bathroom earlier on: real money in the left pocket and fake money in the right pocket.

Carol and Penelope looked really impressed when I bought a pair of jeans for $120.

Carol convinced me to get one of those temporary tattoos when we walked past an Indian lady's stall. I sat for twenty minutes while the woman drew a red cobra on my neck. She told me that it would come right off if I used alcohol. The tattoo looked real cool, and Carol said it made me look dangerous. And that she loved dangerous looking guys.

Next we went into a sneaker store, and Keshawn was trying on sneakers as usual. I was surprised when he spent $320 on two pairs of sneakers. The clerk didn't even notice that the money was fake because he was too busy checking out Carol.

I looked at my watch. It was approaching 4:00 P.M., and I still wanted to see Lila badly. Seeing her would be like adding the cherry on top of a triple scoop vanilla ice-cream sundae.

We gave Carol and Penelope some money to get a cab and told them we would see them at school tomorrow. Carol looked disappointed, and Penelope acted like she didn't want to let go of Keshawn's hand.

He was excited as we sat in the back of our cab. "You see what fun we had today. More fun than we would have had in school." He opened up one of his sneaker boxes. "You got some expensive clothes. I got some expensive clothes. You got your date back. And I got Penelope, the girl who didn't want to be in the same school with me. Didn't I tell you that everything would work itself out?"

I put my hand over my heart. "Good looking on coming through like that. Carol was looking so good that I thought I was going to explode from all the excitement. I wish every day was like this."

We handed the cab driver the money as he stopped in front of my house. He began looking at the money suspiciously.

He started to say something, but when Keshawn gave him a ten dollar tip, he just put the money into his pocket, handed us his card, and told us that if we needed his services again we shouldn't hesitate to call.

"I can't believe it. We broke E Money's rules and still got away with it," I said as we sat on my stoop.

Keshawn had a devilish grin on his face. "Rules are meant to be broken. Especially when you know what you're doing. I planned our day as soon as we got that dough from E Money. Penelope and Carol were the important piece of my master plan."

"Two beautiful women are very distracting to store clerks," he said, still smiling. "Today was a win for them and a double win for us."

I started rummaging through my left pocket and realized all my money was gone. I quickly reached into my right pocket. I pulled out a one dollar bill, a five dollar bill, a ten dollar bill, and four pennies.

I turned to Keshawn and asked, "How much money do you have left?"

He fidgeted in both pockets and came up with seventy-five cents.

"We blew all that money," I said frantically.

"So?" he replied, staring at me. "We can call Christian and get some more. And if he doesn't want to give us any more, we'll go back to E Money's apartment by the end of next week and have him make some for us."

He put his head down as he saw tears rolling down my face.

"End of next week. That's not enough time for me to replace my brother's cello."

"My bad. I didn't think about that. I need to think some things through. I'll catch up with you later."

I didn't answer.

I heard banging on my door. Dennis was telling me that I was going to be late if I didn't get up. I slowly went to the bathroom, went through my regular routine, and left my house. Not seeing Keshawn waiting on my stoop felt weird.

I walked down the block and was about to cross to the other side of the street, avoiding Ms. Reynolds' house, when I saw a black Cadillac Escalade with tinted windows come racing up the block.

I quickly jumped onto the sidewalk. What an idiot.

If I hadn't been paying attention, I would have been road kill.

I was almost at the end of the block when I saw the same black Escalade reverse back down the block and stop right across from me. The back windows came down, and I saw Keshawn's stupid hat.

"I figured things out. Roll with us."

"Who's us?"

The driver side window opened, and I saw Marquis.

"Time is money. And I heard that you need some."

I hesitated at first, but, since I was in a bind and needed money fast, I had to at least see what they were talking about. I slowly opened the back door.

The inside of the SUV was humongous, and I saw Christian sitting shotgun.

"We about to cash a check," he announced.

We drove down Merrick Boulevard. A couple miles later, we found ourselves in front of a cash checking store. Marquis parked around the corner, and we all got out.

Christian looked around suspiciously. "Keshawn, Brandon, why don't you take a walk and get me something to eat. I'll take a bacon, egg, and cheese sandwich on a roll, and get Marquis the same, except replace the bacon with sausage."

I looked at Keshawn and was scolding him with my eyes as we walked up the block.

"They are going to rob the check cashing place," I said, raising my voice.

"I've been with them all morning, and I doubt they are carrying any heat," Keshawn answered calmly.

"How do you know?"

"I have a feeling. Trust me."

"I don't know about your feelings lately. You aren't always right."

"Look, man. If you want to go home, *go*. All I know is that we are going to be getting five thousand apiece. Are you in or not?" he replied, fidgeting with his hat. "Or you could always tell your mama that you broke Dennis' cello. And then you'll see how she'll react when she has to come up with all that bread. I'm not going to let my mom down. We both need a quick come up, and we should be thanking our lucky stars that Christian decided to call me. I need twenty-five hundred by the end of the day, or else the sheriff will be locking up my house. And I told you that I am not living in no projects *ever again*."

"I'm still not sure if I am comfortable with this. My gut feeling is telling me this is going to end up badly."

"This is how you repay me for yesterday? Remember hanging out with Carol and how I orchestrated the hook-up. If you still need to think about this rare opportunity, you can. Take as much time to think all you want. But I am going to get these sandwiches and collect my money."

Keshawn walked off, and I watched from a distance as Christian and Marquis went into the check cashing store.

I caught up with Keshawn. "Okay, I'll follow your lead. I'll be waiting outside the bodega."

It was less than ten minutes before I saw Christian and

Marquis walking up the block.

I wasn't surprised when I heard cop car sirens blaring. Christian and Marquis continued walking at the same pace, and I wondered why they weren't running. What imbeciles. They should at least try to escape, because they were probably going to be spending football numbers behind bars.

I started fidgeting in place, trying to figure out what I should do. What if they told the cops me and Keshawn were with them when they got arrested? I dipped into the store and looked for Keshawn.

"I told you. I told you. The cops just bagged Christian and Marquis," I said as I found him standing by the counter.

He ignored my rant, handed me a ten dollar bill, and calmly said, "Get me two orange juices and pick up the sandwiches. I'm going outside. I'll be right back."

After I paid for the food and drinks, I cautiously walked out of the bodega. Christian, Marquis, and Keshawn were waiting patiently in front of the store for me. Marquis adjusted a book bag on his shoulders, and I noticed Christian was carrying one, too.

What was going on? How come Christian and Marquis weren't in handcuffs?

"You ready to get out of here?" Keshawn asked.

I looked around nervously and spotted two police officers getting out of their patrol car on the other side of the street. They handcuffed a man who appeared intoxicated.

"Some people just don't know how to stay on the right side of the law," Marquis said as he began laughing.

Christian chucked as well. "Don't they know it is better to walk a straight line than a crooked one?"

We all walked back to the car.

After Marquis went through the glove compartment, he said, "I feel like walking. We'll catch up with you guys later."

Christian took off his book bag and gave it to Keshawn then flagged down a dollar van that came roaring down the street.

Keshawn and I walked around the corner.

"You see anyone coming?" he asked.

I carefully surveyed our surroundings, looking east, west, north, and south. We were safe, and Keshawn began looking through the book bag.

At first, it appeared empty, but I was shocked as I began seeing stacks of hundred dollar bills. Before I could say a word, Keshawn's cell phone rang.

"Okay. Got it. I'll speak to you later." He jumped up and down like a grasshopper. "This should take care of your problem. Here you go, sir, fifty big-head Benjamins."

I looked at the money, inspecting it carefully. "This looks and feels just like the real thing."

"It should, because it *is*," he replied, looking around to see if anyone was coming up the block.

"So you want me to take the money they just stole," I said as I continued inspecting the money.

"Wake up, man. If they just stole that money, they would have been arrested. Marquis got the hook up."

"What hook up?"

"Marquis swapped the fake money with the real money at that check cashing place."

"How did he do that without getting caught?"

"His boy works in there, and the manager doesn't check the money too often. Plus, the counterfeit bills are hard to detect thanks to E Money. You know his work is pretty much foolproof."

Brilliant, I thought. I started jumping around like a grasshopper, too, and we both looked strange skipping down the block like two giddy schoolgirls.

We waited about twenty minutes for a bus to arrive and sat in the back. I closed my eyes for a second to relax.

The next thing I remembered was Keshawn shaking me. I looked around as I saw that we were at the bus depot on Jamaica Avenue.

We got off, and he still had the book bag attached to his back.

I was not going to be taken again; I had the cash in different pockets so no one could see any bulges.

Keshawn convinced me to do some shopping. I was not going to blow my second opportunity, so I knew my limit. I had to get Dennis' cello by the end of the day.

We went into a jewelry store and looked around.

I quickly fell in love with a white gold watch with diamonds around the face. I haggled the store owner down to $750. "What happens if I pay cash? "

"That sounds great," the owner said as his eyes lit up. "Since business has been slow and you are paying cash, I will throw in a pair of diamond studded earrings and a diamond studded belt for free."

I gave the store manager another $350, and he gave me a chain and a ring that he said that he was trying to sell for months.

I left the store smiling and thinking that was absolutely the steal of the century. Everyone in school would be feeling sick when they saw all the bling I had.

The next store we went into, I purchased raw denim jeans for $200, a basic white tee, a red sweatshirt that cost me $250, and a pair of limited edition sneakers from Japan, which Keshawn said were the latest style, for $350.

They looked kind of weird to me, but Keshawn knew sneakers. If he said they were hot then I believed most people in school would probably agree.

Next, we went to a check cashing place, where Keshawn paid his light, gas, water, and electricity bills, got the cable turned back on, and paid two months' mortgage in advance. He only had ninety-two dollars left to his name when he left the store.

We passed a barbershop as we walked down the avenue towards the bus stop.

I turned around and convinced him that he needed to get a haircut and get rid of that stupid looking wool hat.

We stepped inside, and everyone was watching Jerry Springer on TV. Tweetie would fit right in; the barbers and some customers began talking to the TV. I wondered if they knew how stupid they looked.

During a commercial, Keshawn took off his hat, and the laughter was so loud that it drowned out the sound of the TV.

The barber, who looked no older than eighteen, was the only one that would touch Keshawn's head.

Keshawn sat in the chair uncomfortably.

"So what kind of cut do you want?" the barber asked, shaking his head back and forth.

"Surprise me," Keshawn said as he looked into the mirror.

That was all the encouragement the barber needed. Forty minutes later, Keshawn's head was an artistic masterpiece. He had a dark Caesar, and the barber cut in little circles on the right side of his head. The barber lined him up so neatly, it looked like it was drawn on. His haircut looked cool.

If Mama hadn't been so conservative, I would have gotten the same thing.

I liked the way the barber cut, but I just played it safe and opted for a dark Caesar with no designs. I wanted to work on my waves, so I bought some wave products that they were selling by the counter. I had to give it a try because I never seemed to be able to get those 360 waves like some people had in my school.

We got on the bus, and Keshawn relished the attention his haircut was getting. It seemed like a quick ride. When we got off the bus, I looked at my watch, and Keshawn did the same.

We ran up the block, and I quickly went inside and put all my new stuff in my closet, under my dirty clothes. That would hopefully deter Dennis and Mama from looking through my stuff.

I hurried back outside, and Keshawn and I waited patiently on my stoop. We weren't saying much.

I looked at my watch for the second time.

"Is that the right time?" he asked, fidgeting on my stoop.

"Yup."

"So where's Lila?"

I had no idea. This wasn't like her at all. Lila was never late before.

"Beats me."

We waited outside for another hour before realizing that Lila wasn't coming. Disappointed, I went inside. As soon as I got to my room, I shut my door.

As I began locking my door, I heard Dennis on the other side, asking to come in. I opened the door.

"Did you get the money for the cello?" he asked, looking around my room.

"Sure did. And they are going to deliver it today."

"For real?"

"Yup. I got a good deal from the violin store in Manhattan, and they threw in an extra string and a sturdier case. Just in case we have another mishap."

Dennis hugged me so hard that I didn't think he was going to let me go.

He finally let me go after I unlocked his grasp around my waist. He turned around and headed out the door with a big smile on his face.

I went back downstairs and looked through the mail. I was happy when I saw a postcard addressed to me from my father.

Hey Brandon,

    I am in Washington. I was listening to this podcast on my iPod by this guy named Tommy Newberry. He said that friends are like elevators, they can take you up or bring you down. I love you and can't wait to see you guys.

Love Dad

    I went to sleep around 12:00 A.M.

    I was awakened briefly at 3:00 A.M. when I heard our car pull up in the driveway.

I woke up as Keshawn threw another rock at my window. I didn't even bother yelling at him because he practically saved my life and I owed him big.

I felt good walking down the block and looking fresh.

Keshawn had on a fly outfit as well. After not seeing his dome in weeks, I was still trying to get used to his peanut head.

"Guess what?" he asked, stroking his head.

"What?"

"I heard Pops' store is open again and he is back on his feet. He didn't suffer any permanent damage and only received a couple of stitches you can hardly see."

"Thank goodness for that."

"I was thinking that we should go play some Super Mario Brothers. I heard the high score is still up."

"No way," I shouted. "I am not in the mood to test any more of your lightning theories."

"All right. Let's just go to school."

It started raining as we waited for the bus. We didn't have umbrellas, and I didn't want to get my new outfit dogged. I was prepared to wait out the rain for however long it took.

A silver Range Rover with tinted windows pulled up in front of the bus stop. The driver started blowing his horn like a madman. The passenger side window went down, and I saw Christian's face.

"You guys want a ride to school? Or you want to stand there and wait out the rain?"

Before I could answer, Keshawn was already opening the back door and motioning for me to get in. I got in and saw Marquis in the driver's seat.

That was the third car I saw Marquis driving, and I wanted to know how many cars he owned.

"Marquis, do you own a dealership?"

He looked at me and chuckled. "I'm like a genie. Whatever I desire, I get it the next day."

Keshawn kicked me in my shin as I was about to ask another question.

When we got to school, Christian told us that he wasn't going in because he had some stuff to take care of.

Keshawn and I got out and ran up the stairs as we heard the first bell ring for homeroom.

I saw Carol in the hallway. She was looking as good as a glass of lemonade on a hot day.

"Nice sneakers, and they are looking right with your outfit," she said as she checked me out.

When Carol noticed my diamond watch, she asked if she could get a closer look. As her hand brushed against mine, I wondered if she saw the goose bumps that began popping up all over my arm.

When the late bell rang, Carol hugged me and said, "Tell Keshawn that Penelope said that she can't wait to see him at lunch."

My swagger was at an all-time high until I reached history class.

Mr. Rogers appeared to be waiting to see my face. "Well, well, well. Look what the cat dragged in. Have you been sick, or did you over sleep the last couple of days?"

I was skating on thin ice and didn't want to be heading back to the principal's office, so I didn't make any confrontational gestures as the class erupted in laughter.

I looked at the board and noticed that there was no DO NOW. I looked on everyone's desk and saw #2 pencils.

We were having a test.

Mr. Rogers never gave multiple choice questions, just short answer questions, which meant there was no way I could guess the answers.

I looked at the questions and started feeling lightheaded. I didn't even bother to write anything on my paper except for my name.

When the period was over, I went to hygiene class. I was confronted with the same thing: Another test and another zero for me. It was shaping up to be the worst day of my academic career. I experienced the same thing in English, biology, and Spanish. I didn't have anything written on any of my tests except for my name.

I thought I was safe when I went to gym class but got a zero for class participation because I didn't have my gym uniform. I sat in the bleachers, thinking I would love to be at home sleeping. I was happy when lunchtime came around. The cafeteria was packed, as usual.

Carol, Keshawn, Penelope, and I sat at the same table, eating fish fillet sandwiches with French fries. I wasn't really focusing on what was going on around me because I was staring into Carol's beautiful brown eyes as we began feeding each other fries.

The period was over quicker than I wanted. When I left the cafeteria, it was as if someone let out all of the air from my balloon.

The day seemed like a bust until Carol kissed me on the cheek as we exited the cafeteria. That's when I knew Cupid wanted to see me smile.

As the eighth period bell rang, I ran to the bathroom on the second floor and changed my clothes. If Mama or even Dennis saw my new stuff, I could be in big trouble, and I didn't want to be on punishment.

When I got home, Mama was already there. I hadn't seen her in a couple of days, and I'd been happy that she hadn't been around to ask where I'd been lately.

She was preparing dinner. "Dennis, Brandon, I have a big surprise when you come back from Mr. Manning's."

I hated surprises. The last surprise we got was when Dad told us that he got a higher paying job. Dennis and I were excited until we found out that he was going to be a truck driver. Nine months later, and I still couldn't forget that surprise.

When Dennis and I got home, we saw an unfamiliar car in the driveway. It was a new black Cadillac sedan, and I wondered who was at our house. I came inside and saw Mama putting the macaroni and cheese on the table.

"Mama, whose car is in the driveway?" I asked, trying to peek in one of the pots she had on the stove.

She gave me *the look*, and I quickly backed away. She hated when I sniffed the pot because she said doing that before it was cooked always messed up the flavors of the food.

She continued going back and forth from the kitchen to the dining room like she didn't hear my question. "I want you and Dennis to wash your hands in the basement and hurry back to the table," she said as she opened the oven.

The sweet smell of Mama's spare ribs had Dennis and me back upstairs in under five minutes.

The dining room table was all fancied up, just like on the TV shows Mama loved to watch in her spare time. She had her fancy table cloth, china plates, crystal glasses, and sterling silverware that she got last year for her wedding anniversary. Everything looked picturesque, including the napkins. I wondered why she was going through all that trouble.

Dennis and I were practically salivating over the spread on the dining table.

"Mama, whose car is that in the driveway?" I asked for the second time, unrolling the napkin and placing it on my lap.

"It's mine," she said as she motioned that I should take

my elbows off the table.

"Mama, that ride is *sweet*," Dennis screamed. "Can you take me to school tomorrow so all my friends can see how we roll?"

"I can't take you."

"Why not?"

I heard the steps creaking and figured Granddad must be back from his excursion. As the shadow turned into the living room, Dennis jumped out of his seat and ran to Dad.

My father was a tall man, standing at about six feet eight inches, and he picked up Dennis in his massive arms like he was holding a baby.

"Surprise! Daddy's home," he said as he put Dennis over his shoulders.

As he put Dennis down, he looked at me. "Boy, get over here and show your father some love."

I didn't know what to do because I was still in disbelief. I wanted him to be home so badly, and now that he was right in front of me, my legs didn't move even though my brain was telling them to.

I finally got it together and slowly approached.

"What's up, Dad?" I said with my hand extended.

"Check out my first born. Come show your father some real love," he said, staring at me like he was seeing me for the first time. "Is that a moustache I see growing in?"

"Daddy, that isn't a moustache. He didn't wash his face this morning," Dennis said as my mother laughed.

I started getting misty eyed as I hugged my father. I didn't want to let go. I was so happy he was back.

"Son, are those tears?"

"Nah, Dad. It's just my allergies," I said, trying to sound convincing.

I guessed everyone in the house had allergies because we were all hugging each other and Mama was crying softly, which was new for her because she usually cried so loud it sounded like someone was attacking her and she was trying to get away.

The food was amazing, and it felt good that we were all under the same roof again.

Mama began telling us about the Cadillac Dad purchased and how she may have to take a class on how to use all the features.

Knowing Mama, it would probably take her a week to figure out how to turn on the navigation alone.

During dessert, Dad made an announcement. "Boys, I am going to be staying home for good. I got a hook-up from one of my clients I delivered for and will be the new manager for this textile factory in New Jersey. I'll be in charge of a hundred and fifty workers on the night shift, starting Monday."

After dessert was finished, I helped Mama clear the table and wash the dishes. Dad and Dennis put away the fancy tablecloth. Then we all gathered in the living room to watch television.

Dennis was sitting real close to Dad. I was on his left side, and Mama was in between his legs. We were munching on popcorn and laughing and joking around just like the good old days.

Mama turned the TV to her favorite station, the National Geographic Channel. They were explaining how animals learned to adapt to their surroundings and survival depended on observing your environment.

During a commercial, Mama said, "Do you mind if we turn on the news?"

Dad replied, "Sure, honey. I want to know what is going on in our city."

As soon as we turned it to the station, across the screen flashed "Breaking news."

As the news reporter talked, I realized that they were broadcasting from my neighborhood.

"...bank robbed for the second time this week by the same person. The police are looking for two suspects. One is a tall male about six feet ten inches, lanky in build, in his mid to late twenties. His accomplice is a male in his early teens, about six feet five inches tall and very muscular in build."

That description sounded like Marquis and Christian.

Dad cranked up the volume.

"More information has just been received. I have been told we have another surveillance tape from the pharmacy across the street from the bank. Please look carefully because the images are grainy. If anyone has seen or recognizes this boy, please contact the police as soon as possible. He is the third accomplice, and authorities think it is possible this young man may have planned the robberies."

I almost swallowed my tongue as I recognized myself on the videotape. As they showed the image again, I breathed a sigh of relief; you couldn't make out my face because of the black hoodie. Thank goodness for the black hoodie over my head, or maybe the cops would be paying me a visit.

Mama and Dad just kept shaking their heads back and forth in disgust.

"I am so blessed to have two law abiding boys. I don't understand why kids don't use their brainpower instead of being so easily led astray," Mama said as she hugged Dennis and rubbed my head.

I excused myself from the living room and went upstairs to my room. I found my black hoodie and the camera I borrowed from Keshawn. I put them in my book bag. As I was about to put the bag under my bed, I heard knocking on my door.

"Come in," I said as I hurriedly put everything under my bed.

My father entered and sat on my bed. "It's good to be home, son."

"It's good to have you back, Dad," I answered

nonchalantly.

"Are you still hanging out with that weird boy, Reshawn? You know what they say about the company you keep, right?"

The guilt was getting to me, and I hope he couldn't detect it on my face.

"Dad, his name is Keshawn, and he's cool. I didn't forget. Show me your company, and I will tell you who you are."

"Sorry, son. Sometimes I get overprotective. You're a big boy now, and I shouldn't worry about you like that anymore. How are your grades?"

"They're coming along real good. Bringing home those A's and a few B's," I said, trying to sound as convincing as possible.

"Why are you lying? It's never good to lie," he said, raising his voice.

"I'm...m not...t...t...t," I stuttered.

"Then maybe I read your last report card wrong."

"You've been snooping in my room," I said loudly. "What about my privacy? You're acting just like Dennis."

"First of all, don't compare me to a child. Secondly, watch your tone. I saw your report card stuffed in the laundry room under the towels. Is that where you're hiding things now? You are the oldest. And when I was gone, you were supposed to be the man of the house. What about setting a good example for your brother? I thought I could count on you to handle your business."

I felt bad letting him down, and his facial expressions told me that he was extremely disappointed.

"Dad, you can count on me. I will make a change, starting right now. I promise I can—no, I *will* do better. Lately things—"

My father stopped me as I continued copping a plea.

"Stop with all that talk. Just show me," he said, still looking disappointed. "Tomorrow starts a new day, and, like Grandma loved to say, the proof is always in the pudding."

He got up and exited my room.

I was left alone with only my thoughts.

I opened my dresser and saw Granddad's favorite book, *Alice's Adventures in Wonderland* by Lewis Carroll, sitting there as if it was telling me to open it.

I turned to the first page and inside read a note from my granddad.

Dear Brandon,

My first grandchild. Full of potential but absent of sight. Open your eyes and you will no longer be blind. Please wake up and stop sleeping your life away before you make your bed so hard that you won't want to lie in it.

Love Always
Granddad

Alice's Adventures in Wonderland was about 140 pages long, and it was the fastest and most interesting book I ever read. When I put it down, it was as if a light bulb came on in my head. I started thinking about my own life.

I could have been in jail but instead I had escaped a bullet that had had my name on it.

I got on my knees and thanked my lucky stars.

Grandma was right, the proof was always in the pudding, and it was time for me to turn over a new page in my life.

I looked over to the corner of my room and saw my notebook. I got up and went over to it and started looking through the pages. Then I did something that I didn't do all year. I began working on all my homework assignments. It was four in the morning when I had them all completed.

I hurried to Mr. Rogers' class as the late bell rang.

As soon as I sat in my seat, he zeroed in on me.

"Good morning, Brandon. You look rested," he said as he opened his grading notebook. "Do you have your homework today?"

"I should have it," I said, opening my book bag.

Everyone in the class started laughing.

"Quiet, class! Let's give him a chance."

I carefully searched through my book bag and found it between my Spanish and English homework. I handed it to him with a smile on my face.

"Congratulations, that's an extra two points for you," he said as he closed his marking book.

When he started a lesson about the Civil War and its key figures, I raised my hand and added some information to his lesson that no one else in the class knew.

"Did aliens abduct you, and your true self was somewhere on Jupiter?" he asked, adding another two points in his grading book.

"Not at all, Mr. Rogers. I am completely awake. My elevator is working and going up to the top floor."

"Well, I don't know when you had this revelation, but keep it up, and maybe you'll pass my class this semester."

"Mr. Rogers, I assure you, the best is to come," I replied as I listened intently while jotting down notes as he continued with his lesson.

I had my academic mojo back, and in each class after that I was a star pupil, even answering questions that the nerds couldn't.

My whole attitude changed, and I remembered the quote my father sent to me in a postcard: "Make your minutes count."

I made my way to the lunchroom. The corridor was unusually noisy. I approached a group of people talking loudly by their lockers. I was in the midst of them and saw Mariah Morgan in the center doing what she did best; performing like the town orator.

"I just heard that Christian Pond got arrested," Mariah announced.

"That can't be right. Christian is cleaner than a whistle," a skinny seventh grader said. Everyone knew she had a serious crush on him. "His parents are rich, and he is way too cute to be so stupid."

"When have I ever been wrong?" Mariah said, twirling her long wavy black hair through her fingers. "My first cousin on my father's side works at the precinct, and they arrested him and his older brother for car theft: They stole a Maserati, a Cadillac Escalade, and a Range Rover, robbed a bank, and confessed to the distribution of counterfeit money."

I moved closer to get more details.

"Christian's brother is definitely older than eighteen, so he'll be going to jail for a long time. I heard for at least ten years. And Christian, he'll be in juvie until he is at least eighteen."

The late bell rang, and I quickly made my way to the cafeteria.

I couldn't stop thinking about Christian and Marquis and what was going to happen to me and Keshawn.

I saw Keshawn in the hallway.

"I already heard. What are we going to do now?" he said, looking as scared as I felt.

"The only thing we can do is keep our fingers crossed."

"I can't believe Marquis and Christian robbed that bank," he said with his head down. "I don't want to go to jail."

"Me, neither," I said, feeling like I was going to throw

up.

Keshawn and I didn't eat lunch and weren't really paying attention to Carol and Penelope as they talked about the upcoming dance at the end of the month.

"What are you wearing, Keshawn?" Penelope asked with a glimmer in her eyes. "I hope your outfit matches mine. I am wearing a pink dress with shoes and bag to match."

"Pink is for girls." He sighed. "I was thinking about wearing blue instead."

Penelope frowned.

"Okay. Okay. If that will make you happy, I'll wear a pink tie but not bright pink."

He always knew what to say, and Penelope blew him a kiss that he caught in mid-air like a centerfielder playing baseball.

Carol turned to me and said, "I am going to be wearing green."

"That's a power color representing money. You should definitely wear a green suit," Keshawn remarked.

I looked at Carol. "If I wore green, I would look like a walking bean pole. I am going to wear black instead."

Carol laughed, and seeing her pretty smile took my mind off Christian and Marquis momentarily.

I got home and couldn't stop thinking about Marquis and Christian snitching on Keshawn and me to get a lighter sentence.

I heard the phone ring but didn't answer. Then I heard cop car sirens and ran to the window to see if they were coming to my house.

I was a nervous wreck, and I kept thinking the jig was almost up and I would be in jail with a cellmate named Bubba.

I went to the phone and called Keshawn. "I'm so

scared. I don't want to go to jail."

"Take it light, homey. There is nothing we could do about it now. I'd rather look on the bright side of things and just go on like nothing happened, because as far as I am concerned nothing did happen."

Wow! Keshawn had nerves of steel, and I guessed he was right; if our fate was sealed then there was nothing we could do about it.

"I am going to speak to you later. I don't think Marquis and Christian will snitch on us. I think they are just going to ride out their jail sentence like some real g's."

I hung up the phone and focused on my new routine. I completed my homework assignments, did some studying, and finished right in time to go outside to catch a glimpse of Lila.

I was sweeping in front of my house, and, as I looked through my peripheral view, I saw Keshawn coming around the corner, sprinting at full speed.

"Did she pass yet?" he asked, breathless.

"Nah."

"That is day number two."

"I know," I said, disappointed. "Let's just wait a little bit longer."

We waited for another hour before we went our separate ways.

TWO MONTHS LATER

The marking period was over, and I was nervous as we received our report cards in homeroom class. I didn't open mine until I got home.

I almost hit the ceiling as I saw that I had an eighty average. My highest grade was from Mr. Rogers, who gave me an eight-five.

My family and I went out to celebrate at a fancy Italian restaurant in Manhattan later on that night.

Mama and Dad were in rare form.

"This is to my brilliant boys," Mama said as we toasted with sparkling cider."I am so proud of the both of you."

Dad seemed like he had his speech all planned out. He took out a piece of paper and read it slowly. "Life is such a beautiful thing when you take the blinders off. See, hear, think, and do, in one accord, and everything will fall into place like touched dominos."

That was a special night and one that I would always remember.

I awoke to Keshawn throwing rocks at my window again. I got dressed and met him outside.

"The dance is coming up soon," he said. "Did you buy your suit?"

"Nah. Not yet. I don't have any money."

"Me, neither."

He gave me a look, and I knew he was thinking of a new scheme.

"I've got an idea," he said, with a crooked smile on his face. "Peep this. I want to set up an eBay account and get people to buy things. And when the money gets transferred into an account I set up, I will withdraw the cash and close it out...after giving the customers the runaround about their purchases being on their way."

I gave him the evil eye. "I don't need to think too hard. That's not a good idea."

"You thinking now? Are you chicken or what? You've changed since Christian and Marquis got busted. That was two months ago, and we didn't take the rap for anything. I told you that they wouldn't snitch on us. What could happen? Don't tell me that you're scared?"

"Scared? I'm not *scared*. Try *being aware*. We could have been facing some serious time if we had gotten busted. No thanks. You are on your own. I'd rather ask my parents for the money."

"You know you aren't going to get it," Keshawn said with a smirk on his face. "*You owe me*. Or do I have to remind you about all that I've done for you."

"All you've done? I've been asleep for the longest. Not doing my schoolwork, happy with failing grades. Doing stupid things with you that can affect my future. I've been

145

living in a fantasy land, just like Alice in the book *Alice's Adventures in Wonderland*. Well, I've found my way home, and I don't want to jump down any more rabbit holes."

"Rabbit holes?"

This was my opportunity to school Keshawn. "See, the rabbit hole is a metaphor for going on an adventure into the unknown. Alice went down one because of boredom, not thinking about what was going to happen. She had to go through all these tests and meet unusual characters who taught her stuff so that she could get herself back home. She learned a lot of things during that adventure," I said, slowly exhaling. "Life lessons, my father calls them. She almost lost her life at the end, but she found out that she was dreaming. Sleeping. Well, I am not sleeping anymore. I am always going to be on the lookout. I'm not jumping down any rabbit holes. Especially with you. You can jump down any rabbit hole you want by *yourself*."

"I'm impressed. I never read that novel," he said, looking up the block. "Last chance. Are you in or what? We can make mad paper."

"Nope. You can do what you want. But count me out."

It felt good telling him no. I survived my rabbit hole and felt grateful that I was able to chalk up my adventure as a learning experience, not one that got me locked up like Christian and Marquis.

At lunchtime, I saw Keshawn sitting with Penelope and Carol. As I approached, I felt like I wasn't welcome as I spoke to Carol and Penelope and they ignored me. I felt totally disrespected. I put my tray down next to Keshawn.

"Yo, I was thinking, I'm not feeling your new philosophies. It's like I don't even know who you are anymore," he said, staring at me long and hard.

Penelope and Carol didn't even look in my direction and were still acting like I wasn't around.

I was fuming, but then I remembered what Dad wrote on one of his postcards: "Friends are like elevators; they can bring up or take you down."

I wasn't willing to jump down any more rabbit holes. I ate my lunch in the far end of the cafeteria by myself.

While everyone was outside running up and down, I did something unusual. I went to my guidance counselor Mr. Feldman and asked him what high schools I would be able to get into.

He usually had the same stoic look on his face, and I couldn't tell what he was thinking. He kept looking through my records, which he had in a folder on his desk then peeking up at me. He did this for about ten minutes before calmly stating, "Well, Mr. Stewart, I don't know what to say to you about your high school choices. I don't think you'll be able to even graduate this year without going to summer school, and that is if you pass all your classes plus all your state tests in English, math, history... Your grades are—let's say, not in the top ten percent of your class."

I left his office feeling disappointed, and, as I made my way to my next class, I realized I had no one to blame but myself.

I got on the bus, and it felt weird sitting by myself, but Granddad always said, "Being a man is taking responsibility for yourself."

I rang the bell when I saw a crowd of people standing in front of Pops' store. Police officers were coming in and out of his store, carrying boxes of stuff, and Pops was in the back of a squad car. When our eyes made contact, Pops just slouched back into his seat, seeming ashamed that I saw him.

I stood around hoping that, out of the crowd of people hanging around, someone would spill the beans. As luck would have it, a middle age lady was broadcasting like a news reporter.

"They finally caught up to Pops. Running numbers and gambling. He wasn't licensed to do that, and anyone with any sense in their heads knows that's illegal."

Simon Chase, the running back for my school's football team, chimed in. "Doesn't the government do the same thing? But they call it Lotto. They should be arresting the government, too. What about Las Vegas? Taking people's money. How many people win anything at those casinos?"

The old lady just shook her head. "Before you play any game, you should know the rules, young man. What's good for the goose isn't necessarily good for the gander."

Simon walked off as she continued talking to an elderly gentleman. "I hope he saved his money. He's going to need a good lawyer. The law doesn't play when they catch your hand in the cookie jar."

I looked at Pops in the patrol car and saw tears rolling down his face. I remembered Pops giving us that sermon about sleeping. He was also sleeping, and he would probably have to pay for his transgressions by spending a couple years in jail.

I didn't want to stick around longer and began slowly walking home.

I got inside, and the first thing I did was complete all my homework assignments. I was finished and looked at my clock. It was 4:00 P.M.

I waited outside for over an hour for Lila and realized that she wasn't coming. I came back inside and took a nap.

I awoke to Dennis knocking on my door. "You got a phone call."

"Who is it?"

"I am not your secretary. Come find out yourself. But don't worry, it isn't a girl. You know none of those call here."

I came downstairs and picked up the phone. "Hello," I said, not hearing anyone on the other end. "Hello. Hello."

"Hello," an unfamiliar voice said.

"Who is this? I don't have time for games."

"It's me, Keshawn."

He didn't sound like Keshawn. He sounded like he had been crying or had lost his voice.

"I apologize for cutting you off like that. That was immature. We boys for life, right, no matter what," he said as I heard him sniffle a couple times. "I decided not to do any more scams."

"Are you sure I am speaking to the same Keshawn?" I replied, surprised. He rarely changed his mind.

"I read *Alice's Adventures in Wonderland* at the library and realized what you were saying. Thinking things completely through can force me to make better decisions, because I may be making a choice that will affect me forever," he said, dragging his words. "But I still feel bad for Christian and Marquis, though. Somehow, we got lucky, and they didn't."

"Yeah. We can definitely thank our lucky stars."

I saw Carol and Penelope in the hallway as I made my way to Mr. Rogers' class. I figured they were more trouble than they were worth, and I didn't make any eye contact with them.

I came into the classroom, and Mr. Rogers had a big Kool-Aid smile on his face. I returned his smile and thought to myself how quickly things changed.

Everyone was seated, and Mr. Rogers became deadly serious. "Class, I am handing back your test scores from two days ago. And I am not satisfied with the grades. Am I wasting my time trying to teach you that history connects you with the world and your surroundings?"

As he handed the papers back, I saw a lot of blue faces. When I received mine, I flipped it over to discover a hundred.

I couldn't keep it in. "That's what I am talking about," I said as I pumped my fist in the air.

Mr. Rogers continued handing back the papers. "Mr. Stewart had the highest test score in the class. I wish everyone else understood the information like he did. He is a model student and one many of you could learn from."

I never imagined in a zillion years that the nerds in my class would be jealous of me. I was bugged out when a couple of the nerds approached after class ended.

"Brandon, if you ever have a study group, can you *please* invite us? We are willing to pay you top dollar to be a part of it."

"If I do, I'll keep you guys in mind," I replied as I chuckled inside.

If Keshawn had been there, he would have definitely taken them up on their money offer.

At lunchtime, I barely touched the baked chicken, which usually tasted like rubber. I was sipping on some chocolate milk when I saw my parents enter with Principal Jones.

Gossip Queen Mariah Morgan saw what was going on and pointed Principal Jones to the table where I was sitting.

As they headed in my direction, Keshawn looked like he saw a ghost. He started inching away from me, and before I knew it he was at the other end of the table.

Everyone in the lunchroom became quiet, and I heard Mama's squeaky shoes as she walked across the cafeteria floor. She still had on her scrubs, and Dad's wrinkled forehead told me that he had a lot on his mind. He only did that when he was in deep thought.

Principal Jones cleared his throat before speaking. "Brandon, please follow me back to my office."

My parents were next to him but weren't even acknowledging my existence. This was a bad sign. Silence meant something was wrong, and I didn't need to be a rocket scientist to figure out I was the one who I was up to my neck in trouble.

When we got to his office, Principal Jones began talking to my parents. "Mr. and Mrs. Stewart, you can sign him out. I hope everything works itself out."

I had never heard Principal Jones be so cryptic.

I sat in the backseat as we headed up the block, away from school. It was church quiet, and Dad had both hands on the wheel like he was concentrating on passing his driver's test and didn't want to break any laws. Mama was staring off into space.

"Dad, what's going on?"

Before he could answer, Mama let out a loud wail. "Why, son? Why? Where have I gone wrong?" she said as she folded her hands together like she was praying.

Dad pulled the car over to the side of the road and rocked her back and forth in his arms.

"Don't worry, honey. Everything will be okay."

"Okay?" she said between sniffles. "Nothing will ever be okay. His life is ruined." She turned her gaze to me and started shaking her head back and forth as my father continued trying to console her.

My father turned the engine back on and looked at her. "What precinct do we have to go to again?"

I wanted to cry. My luck ran out, and the jig was finally up. I knew Christian and Marquis weren't going to take the rap for everything. But how come they didn't tell on Keshawn? He was a part of it, too.

I slouched in the backseat, feeling hollow inside.

We parked in the precinct parking lot.

"Brandon," my mother said slowly as my father held her hand.

My thoughts were moving in an uncontrollable whirlwind. "Yes," I said, feeling ashamed.

"Dennis got arrested," she replied as she squeezed my father's hand.

"Dennis…s," I stuttered. "For what?"

"I don't know all the charges, honey. Something about trying to pass off counterfeit money in a store, defrauding the country, and…"

We got inside the precinct, and Dad inquired about Dennis' whereabouts. It seemed like he was getting the runaround. My father continued badgering the officer.

"I have a right to see my son. What is taking so long? I need to see him *now*."

"Sir, if you do not watch your tone and have a seat, you will have to leave." The officer appeared to be in no hurry. "We will find out where your son is. Just relax."

Dad reluctantly had a seat next to me.

Mama was on the phone with a lawyer because my Aunt Phyllis—who lived in Florida and whose kids (my first cousins) were always having trouble with the law—said that Dennis' goose would be cooked if he didn't have any legal representation.

An hour passed before an officer told my parents that they could see Dennis. I couldn't wait to see him, too, but I was instructed to stay put.

I sat on the cold bench with only my thoughts.

It was a quiet ride home. I sat next to Dennis, and he didn't even look at me.

Mama was upset. "Dennis, where did you get that money from? I thought you knew better than that. I would never expect something like this from you."

Dennis didn't utter a word.

Dad interrupted Mama as she asked Dennis where he got the money for the second time.

"This desk appearance ticket they gave me in the precinct says that we have to go to Family Court a month from now to see what happens next. We have to make sure that we do all we can to help him."

When we got inside, I went to my room while my parents discussed their options in the kitchen.

I knocked on Dennis' door.

"Can you forgive me? I didn't mean for any of this to happen," I said.

He had his head buried in his pillow on his bed. "That's how you treat your own flesh and blood?" he said, uncovering his face and looking at me in disgust. "Why didn't you tell me that you gave me counterfeit money?"

How could I explain my stupidity? I was ashamed of myself. I put my head down.

"I didn't leave you out in the cold like you did to me," he said, sitting upright. "I didn't tell on you because blood is always thicker than water. Hopefully, they won't put me in jail for long."

"I don't want you to go to jail for me."

"Too late now. You should have been thinking about all that stuff before. Maybe they will dismiss my case when they see my clean record, good grades, et cetera. Because if they find out it is was you, and being that you are older, you'll probably be going to juvie much longer than I would."

I didn't know what to say and went downstairs and called Keshawn.

He was surprised to hear my voice.

I told him everything, and he said calmly. "My name didn't come up, right?"

"Nah."

"Cool."

"Cool? My brother got arrested and has to go to court, and all you can say is *cool*. This is our problem, too." He didn't sound concerned about me or my brother. He actually seemed happy that his name wasn't caught up in all this drama

"I didn't mean it that way. I was just asking a question. Let me come up with a plan that will get the both of you out of this situation. I got to go."

TWO WEEKS LATER

I hadn't heard from or seen Keshawn ever since I'd told him that Dennis had gotten busted.

School became uncomfortable as well. Mariah Morgan told everyone in school what the deal was with my brother, and no one wanted to come near me.

Dinner, which was usually loud, now became a time of silence. Everything changed at my house since Dennis got arrested.

Especially the food. Fried chicken, macaroni and cheese, and collard greens—one of Mama's specialties— didn't taste the same. It was salty and burnt. Mama never burned a meal for as long as I could remember, and the bags under her eyes told me that she wasn't sleeping much.

I reluctantly ate, and Dad and Dennis didn't make a big deal about it, either. After I washed the dishes, Mama began cleaning the house like she was expecting the president or something.

I was assigned to clean all the bathrooms, and I made sure that my room was cleaner than a hospital.

Mama said, "Dennis, go wash up and get ready for your interview."

"Mama, what interview?" I asked.

"Child Protective Services is coming to interview Dennis before his court date."

It was five o'clock when I heard the doorbell ring.

"Brandon, get the door," Mama yelled from upstairs.

I was surprised to see Lila standing there. It had been a

157

while, and I wondered why she was knocking on my door.

"Hi, Lila," I said, taking in her perfume.

"Can I come in?"

I hesitated. "This isn't a good time. We are expecting company."

"I'm the company, silly. I have to interview your brother. I work with CPS now."

I let Lila in and escorted her to the living room.

My parents were all dressed up like they were going to a job interview. Dennis was sitting at the table with a suit and tie on. He had his hands folded in front of him like a little angel.

Mama offered Lila a drink.

"No, thank you, ma'am. Do you mind if we get straight down to business?"

"Sure," my mother replied.

"I need to talk to Dennis alone. I hope you don't mind. It's just procedure."

My parents passed off a fake smile and headed upstairs. I pretended to go to the basement. I wanted to hear everything that was going on.

"Hi, Dennis. I'm Lila Johnson. But you can call me Lila, if you like."

"That's a pretty name. For a pretty girl."

I heard Lila giggle, and I wondered where my brother learned to sweet talk girls.

"Do you like living here?"

"I wouldn't change it for the world. My parents are the best."

"Do your parents beat you?"

"No, I have never been beaten in my life."

"Are your parents having money problems?"

"Not that I know of."

"Are you having issues at school?"

"No, I love school. I am a straight A student."

"How does your brother treat you?"

"He's the best brother in the world."

"Where did you get that money from?"

I didn't hear Dennis answer.

"Dennis, did you hear my last question?"

"Yeah."

"You do know that what you did was a serious offense. Something that can't be taken lightly. You can trust me. Just be honest and tell me where you got that money from."

Dennis still didn't respond.

"Are you protecting someone?" Lila asked in a more serious tone.

Thoughts were coming from everywhere, and I started playing out scenarios in my head. If Dennis got convicted, he'd probably get probation. But if I were to admit to everything, I'd probably be stuck in juvie for a while.

I heard Lila's voice rise. "Dennis, you need to answer my question. We need to know. If not, I can't help you, and you'll be at the mercy of the court system."

Dennis began sniffling, and he only did that right before he cried.

I felt terrible.

I came flying into the room.

"It was my money," I said as my heart pounded in my chest. "I gave it to him. He didn't know. He was trying to protect me."

"Brandon, I am surprised. So, so surprised," Lila said, looking shocked. "I thought you were a good kid."

The look on Lila's face made me feel like dirt. When my parents came back downstairs, she explained to them what happened. Mama fell to the floor, holding her face in her hands, and Dad was in such a shocked state he demanded that I repeat what I said.

"Dad, it was my money. I am sorry. I didn't mean for any of this stuff to happen."

I thought my father was going to tear my head off.

If Lila hadn't reminded him that beating me would only have made the situation worse, he would have knocked me into next year.

Lila told my parents that she would report her findings to the court and didn't see why Dennis would be charged. She didn't seem to have the same confidence in my situation and told my parents they should get a lawyer.

As Lila left, Mama got on the phone with a lawyer. After explaining to him that I confessed to having counterfeit money, he recommended that we allow the authorities to interview me.

I didn't think things would move so quickly, but we got a phone call from the cops an hour later. The interview was to be held tomorrow at 4:30 P.M.

The day flew by, and I didn't see Keshawn in school. I went to his house and knocked on his door, but no one was there, so I went home.

At 4:25, the doorbell rang. Two police officers were at the door. My father let them in and escorted them to the living room.

I felt stupid in my suit and tie, but Mama told me our lawyer said I should try to make a good first impression.

"Hello, young man. I am Officer Sanchez, and this is Officer White."

"Hello, Officer Sanchez and Officer White," I replied as they stared at me intensely.

Officer White said, "We need to know where you got that money from. You can be charged with several infractions, including possession of a forged instrument. What you did was a federal crime."

I didn't want to go to jail, and I didn't want to snitch on anyone. I didn't respond.

"Look, young man. Don't waste our time. It will be your butt behind in jail. Not ours."

Jail wasn't anyone's intentional vacation spot. I was up the creek without a paddle.

"So what's it going to be, young man," Officer Sanchez said.

I took a deep breath. I knew what I had to do. I had to take responsibility for my actions, just like Mama was telling me to do for years.

"I got it from this guy name E Money in his Grandma Tweetie's apartment," I said, talking like I just unloaded something heavy from my shoulders.

"Nicknames aren't that helpful. Give us some real

names and a location."

"It was in Baisely Projects."

After the cops got the building and apartment number, they told me they would have to check out my story and get back to me.

When they left, I called Keshawn. I was happy when he picked up the phone on the fourth ring.

"Where you been?" I asked.

"I was down south for a little while."

"For what?"

"Are you the cops or something? Why you so nosey all of a sudden?"

"The cops just interviewed me."

"The cops? Why would they be speaking to you?"

"I told them about E Money and Tweetie."

I heard silence on the phone.

"Did you mention my name?"

"Nah. And so what if I did? Boys for life, right?"

"Of course. If you need to give the cops my address, go ahead. I will tell them everything. I got your back for life. Ride or die."

I felt good that Keshawn was riding for me.

TWO DAYS LATER

Officer Sanchez and Officer White came back to the house, and I was wearing the same stupid suit and tie.

"We checked out your story, and we didn't find any E Money, Ernest, or Tweetie at the address you gave us."

"Are you sure?"

"Look, son, we don't have time to play games with you. Lying won't help. Do you have anyone else to corroborate your story?"

"My friend, Keshawn. He lives around the corner. He was there with me," I replied frantically.

Both officers left and came back roughly an hour later.

Officer Sanchez said, "We spoke to Keshawn. And he said that he didn't know anything about E Money, Ernest, Tweetie, Baisely Projects, or counterfeit money. He also said that he had hardly spoken to you in a while."

I felt betrayed.

"How about calling these two girls Penelope and Carol?" I said frantically. "Keshawn and I gave them money and took them shopping."

The officers looked like they were at their wits' end.

Officer White said, "Look, young man. We don't have time to check out every one of your leads. Nothing you told us has panned out. You are going to have to plead your case when you have your day in court."

They gave my parents a DAT. When Mama read it, she began crying.

The court date was set for a month later.

Being inside a courtroom wasn't what I expected. While it looked so glamorous on the TV, reality was the total opposite. The air seemed thick, and I felt like I was suffocating. The judge peered over at me and my lawyer, while the prosecutor looked at us like a ravenous coyote.

She was a skinny blonde lady who looked like she worked out seven days a week and locking up criminals was just a hobbyfor her..

My lawyer, Mr. Aldridge, on the other hand, looked like he was ready to go to sleep and was sweating so much I wondered if he ever tried a case before.

The judge looked at the prosecutor. "You may call your first witness."

As if on cue, the prosecutor stood up and said, "The People call Carol Whittaker."

I looked around to see the court officer leading Carol into the courtroom. She was looking like quite the perfect angel in her business suit and her round rim glasses. She was really putting on an act.

After she was sworn in by the clerk, she readied herself to begin answering the prosecutors questions.

"Good morning, Ms. Whittaker. My name is Ms. Cleaver. I'm going to ask you a few questions. If I ask you something that you don't understand, feel free to let me know, and I'll try my best to ask my questions in a clearer manner, okay?"

"Okay," Carol replied, looking completely relaxed.

Ms. Cleaver stood up and began her questioning. She started by asking Carol some personal background questions like where she lived and went to school.

Though that all seemed simple enough, I felt lost during

the proceedings. I knew the judge, prosecutor, and Carol were speaking English, but I still couldn't understand most of their terminology.

Because of this, it was all beginning to get quite boring until the Ms. Cleaver asked Carol, "Do you know a person by the name of Brandon Stewart?"

Carol answered, "Yes, I do."

"If you see that person in the court room, could you point to him and identify an article of clothing that he is wearing?" Ms. Cleaver said.

Carol readied herself, turned toward me, pointed, and said, "Yes, that's him over there. He's wearing that metallic blue tie with a matching blue shirt."

Judge Benson suddenly spoke. "Indicating the defendant."

Ms. Cleaver continued her line of questioning. She seemed to cover every single detail of the incident in question.

Then she asked a question that made my heart skip a beat. "Did you think it was strange that Brandon had so much money?"

"To be honest, I did think it was funny that Brandon had so much money, and he was spending it like crazy," Carol calmy answered.

"Were you alone with him?"

"No, my friend Penelope Cunningham was also there."

What a big fat liar. What about Keshawn? Was this a conspiracy against me?

I felt like Alice sinking deep into a rabbit hole. I just wanted to make my way home.

I looked at my lawyer as he scribbled some notes on his notepad.

When Ms. Cleaver finished, Judge Benson said, "Mr. Aldridge, you may cross examine the witness."

I looked at him and watched as a stream of sweat came running down his face and onto his chin.

Judge Bension became irritated. "Mr. Aldridge, you may now cross examine the witness."

He took out a handkerchief from his pocket and started wiping his face. It was then that I noticed that his hands were shaking.

"Is it hot in here?" he asked me,

"No," I responded, wondering when he was going to get up and defend me.

Judge Benson spoke even louder. "Mr. Aldridge, are you going to cross examine the witness? We don't have all day."

"No, Your Honor, that won't be necessary at this time."

I sat and watched in utter disbelief as Ms. Cleaver called several other people, many of whom I did not know. I did recognize Penelope's face and listened as she offered the same rehearsed testimony that Carol gave earlier on.

This was not going as I envisioned it. My whole world was crumbling in front of my eyes.

I leaned over and whispered into Mr. Aldridge's ear. "What are you doing? Is everything going okay?"

He smiled. "Don't worry, I got this. Ms. Cleaver is just posturing for the judge."

After the prosecution rested its case, it was finally our turn. I was ready to see Mr. Aldridge put on a show; my aunt said his nickname was The Destroyer.

Any minute, he'd be shooting down the prosecution's case like pitching pennies in a fountain. As he began getting up, I wondered how many witnesses he was going to call to the stand.

The wait was short lived. Mr. Aldridge had other plans. My lawyer, if you can call him that, did not call one witness in my defense. The only thing he managed to say was, "The defense rests, Your Honor."

The judge looked at my lawyer and said, "Then, Mr. Aldridge, you may now proceed with your closing statements."

Mr. Aldridge smiled. He looked like he was ready to tear Ms. Cleaver to shreds. I felt relieved. This had to be the time where he was about to tell the judge about me and how justice demanded that all the charges should be dropped.

"No, Your Honor. I will not be providing a closing statement." He quickly sat down.

"That's it? That's your big plan? Shouldn't you say something else in my defense?" I said, looking at him like he just lost his mind.

"It's not required in your case. Don't worry. This case will be over in two shakes of a hand. You will be in the comfort of your home before you know it. The burden of proof always lies on the prosecutor. Their case isn't strong enough for any serious time to be issued. You're a good kid who just got caught up in a bad situation, right?"

"I guess so," I reluctantly answered.

Judge Benson announced, "Ms. Cleaver, you may begin your closing statement."

I could swear I saw her lick her lips in anticipation.

Then she stood up for the last time and said, "Thank you, Your Honor."

She went on and on for an hour and a half. By the end, I felt like the room actually shrank in size. I felt a massive headache coming on.

I was sweating as she continued. "Your Honor, the People have proven, beyond a reasonable doubt, that Brandon Stewart, knowingly and with intent to defraud, exchanged a quantity of counterfeit U.S. currency on April 8, 2009, at around 10:00 a.m. I will ask that you hold him accountable for the crime of Criminal Possession of a Forged Instrument in the First Degree."

My parents looked disgusted. Mama rubbed her rosary beads back and forth in her hands. Dad's forehead was all wrinkled up. He seemed nervous—as was I.

"We are going to take a recess until after lunch," Judge Benson announced as he looked at his watch.

Five hours later, everyone was back in the courtroom.

Judge Benson said, "Having heard all the evidence in this trial, I am now prepared to present my findings of fact and issue a verdict in this matter."

Mr. Aldridge winked when I looked in his direction, as if to say there was nothing to worry about.

"I find..." Judge Benson said, "...all the evidence presented against Brandon Stewart credible, and accordingly find him guilty of all the counts charged."

The word guilty felt like a bullet penetrating my skin.

"We need to discuss sentencing," Judge Benson said, looking at me. "Mr. Aldridge, are there any members of his family present?"

My parents raised their hands, and the judge asked if one of them would come to the bench.

Mama slowly walked past me and shook her head when our eyes met. I could see the disappointment on her face. She was still clutching her rosary beads.

"I have a question for you," Judge Benson said, looking at my mother with pity.

"Yes, Your Honor," she replied, looking like all the air was let out of her balloon.

"I am not saying what I am going to do, but if I were to send Brandon home, would you be able to supervise him? Specifically have him adhere to a strict curfew and be part of some positive extracurricular activities that foster responsible actions? Would you be able to see that he does these things?"

Mama was still clutching to her rosary beads. I heard her clear her throat, and I was expecting the word "Yes" to come out at any minute. This was my get out of jail free card, and I wanted to jump for joy.

She cleared her throat a second time, but still no words came out of her mouth.

Judge Benson looked perplexed. "Ma'am, did you understand my question?"

Mama still didn't answer, and I wondered why she was getting all choked up.

I had never known her to have a loss of words.

She turned around and looked at me long and hard, as if she was searching through my soul.

My eyes were telling her to tell the judge yes because I learned my lesson and wanted to put this whole experience behind me.

Mama turned back to the judge and took in a deep breath. "Your Honor, to tell you the truth, I don't think I'll be able to monitor him. Brandon doesn't listen to me. This is obvious, being that we are even in court for such a stupid and foreseeable outcome. I have been telling him to be responsible and focus for as long as he has been on this earth. But my father always said—and I've even heard him say it to Brandon—that 'a hard head makes for a soft behind.' Do with him what you want. Maybe he will learn from this experience. Because I am at my wits' end."

Was everyone crazy except me?

What was Mama thinking, throwing me to the wolves like that? I looked on in shock, and my father seemed to somehow agree with her.

"Thank you for your candid response, Ma'am," Judge Benson said.

Mr. Aldridge looked like a deer caught in headlights, and Ms. Cleaver was hiding a smile that appeared to want to erupt at any second.

Judge Benson continued. "I have decided to remand you to the custody of a group home for juvenile delinquents for six months. Young man, I see kids like you every day, not being responsible. Hoping that by saying sorry or by seeing the error in your ways after you get caught is somehow acceptable. Thinking you have all the time in the world to get focused. That's not always the case, and I hope you end up a better man from this experience. You have no one to blame but yourself."

When his gavel hit his desk, I knew my life would never be the same. My whole body went numb as the court officers began to circle me like vultures around a carcass.

When they handcuffed me and took me away, all I could do was hang my head down in shame. *I hope I can survive this,* I thought.

I didn't like being handcuffed on the bus with other kids and wearing a stupid white outfit. I felt like a true criminal and knew it was going to be a long ride upstate. I didn't know what to expect. I saw some kids sleeping, but I couldn't close my eyes.

I didn't want to ever sleep again. I didn't know what to expect. I looked around again and I saw a boy two rows back who reminded me of Keshawn. I started getting angry. Keshawn wasn't my boy, he was a poser. I hated him. I began getting even madder, but I calmed down as one of Mama's many sayings popped into my head.

"You have to take responsibility for your own actions."

I looked through the window and I could swear I saw a rabbit running across a field as we sped down the throughway. I wondered if he was searching, avoiding, or going down a rabbit hole.

That decision had already been made for me.

And something I realized all too late. If you fall asleep in the game of life and follow others instead of yourself, you will have no one to blame but yourself in the end.

I closed my eyes for a minute and began thinking about the horrifying stories I heard about being in a group home. I heard that a group home was a prelude to the real thing. I wasn't built for any of this stuff.

Granddad always said, "You pay for everything you do, good or bad, one way or another." He was right. I was learning my life lesson with my *freedom*—one of the greatest gifts you can have.

We arrived in Syracuse, New York, at 10 P.M., and, after being treated like the property of New York State, I found myself in a room with two other boys. I had the top bunk, and the mattress was hard and lumpy, not like the soft mattress I had in my own room at home.

The lights went out, and I lay awake, thinking about this rabbit hole I had to endure for the next six months.